CHAMPION
Studs in Spurs

Cat Johnson

Copyright © 2017 Cat Johnson

All rights reserved.

ISBN-13: 978-1545459416
ISBN-10: 154545941X

DEDICATION

For all the readers who have welcomed me and my bull riders into their lives.

STUDS IN SPURS

Unridden
Bucked
Ride
Hooked
Flanked
Thrown
Champion
Spurred
Wrecked

CHAPTER ONE

Ten years ago

"Coop." Glen leaned into the living room from the kitchen doorway. "We're outta beer."

"We can't be." Cooper eyed the four empty bottles on the table next to him. Two were his and two belonged to the girl he'd brought home. "We had like two twelve-packs last I looked."

"Yeah, we did. Yesterday. We're all out now." Glen hooked a thumb toward the kitchen. "Go look for yourself if you don't believe me. The fridge is empty."

Cooper wasn't sure it was worth the effort to get off the sofa and out from under the woman draped across his lap. But if his business partner and best friend was correct in his evaluation of the beer situation, one of them had to go out and get more, and it didn't look like Glen was offering.

That Glen was shirtless, barefoot and wearing nothing but boxer shorts told Cooper he'd most likely been naked just moments before. It would be easier for Cooper to run out since he was still dressed, right down to his boots.

Well, he was dressed except that his belt was undone and the fly on his jeans hung wide open. He hadn't bothered to fix any of that, figuring it would be a waste of time. The woman next to him on the sofa didn't seem like she was near done with him yet.

It was still early for a Saturday night. If they really were out of beer, that meant they wouldn't have any for the remainder of the weekend and wouldn't be able to buy more. He wasn't riding tomorrow, so he'd definitely be drinking.

Stupid ass, archaic liquor laws. This was the new millennium. He would think in this day and age a man would be able to purchase a damn six-pack on a Sunday if he wanted.

The alcohol laws in Arkansas were tough and random, depending on where you were. Coop supposed he should be grateful he didn't live in one of the many totally dry counties in this state.

Coop's final deciding factor as to whether or not to get up and go get beer was that he needed a little recovery time the girl next to him didn't seem to want to give. Just a few minutes ago, she'd sucked him off, yet her hands had still been all over him when Glen had walked in and interrupted her.

A man Coop's age, and one who'd consumed a bit of beer, could use maybe an hour to get revved up again for round two. Hell, at least half an hour would be nice.

"I'll go." Cooper braced one hand against the arm of the sofa and hoisted himself from beneath the girl.

"A'ight. Get enough for tomorrow too since it's Sunday."

"I know." Coop scowled at Glen. "Why the hell do you think I'm going tonight?"

"Just checking. You okay to drive?" Glen eyed him more closely.

"Yeah, I'm fine." He'd built up a good tolerance over the years. It took more than a couple of beers consumed over a span of hours to get him drunk.

"Okay." Glen spun and headed back to his bedroom where he had a tidbit of his own waiting for him.

"You coming, darlin', or you staying here?" Cooper asked

his companion for the evening as he zipped his fly and buckled his belt.

She'd sucked his cock like a champ, but he'd be damned if he could remember her name at the moment. It had something to do with a bird. Or maybe a tree or a bush. Lily? Laurel?

Lauralee. That was it. Damn proud of himself for having pulled that information out of his ass, he waited for her answer.

"I think I'll stay and take a little nap while you're gone." Her eyelids were drooping pretty low.

He'd bet the winning payout at the next event that she'd be asleep in two minutes. Unlike him, Lauralee looked both tired and tipsy. He had a feeling his companion would be staying the night, unless Glen finished with her friend and she could drive them both home.

The damn waif of a girl likely weighed all of ninety pounds. No wonder a couple of beers had her falling asleep. He didn't even feel buzzed from the ones he'd had. But then again, he had bought her and her friend a shot or two back at the bar.

That had probably done her in. The hard stuff hit women harder than it did men.

He looked down at her curled up with her bare legs tucked beneath her, her slender arms wrapped around a throw pillow. Her tits were practically nonexistent. She was too skinny, in his opinion.

When had women stopped wanting to look like women? The magazine covers by the cash register at the store always featured models and actresses who were nothing but skin and bones. She was sweet and pretty enough, but Cooper preferred his females with a nice handful of curves on them, not these chicks with their ribs and hip bones sticking out.

Beggars couldn't be choosers, he supposed. This was an off-week for him. He wasn't competing in any bull-riding events this weekend. Without the plethora of buckle bunnies hanging around the chutes at the arena looking for attention and throwing themselves at the riders, pickings for companionship could be slim. He and Glen had been lucky to land these two at the local bar.

"A'ight. I'll be back in a few." Feeling in the pocket of his jeans, he found his wallet right there where he'd left it.

"Okay." She gave him a halfhearted wave and closed her eyes.

As he scooped the truck keys off the table by the door, he had a feeling she wouldn't miss him all that much while he was gone.

The trip to the store, only a couple of miles down the road, took all of five minutes. They charged more for everything than at the bigger chains, but this place was convenient.

A little too convenient sometimes, if you asked him. To be able to run out and buy beer within two miles of his house meant they probably did it more often than they should. If he'd had to drive the half hour each way to the MegaMart, he wouldn't be going. Not at this hour and after the beers he already had in him, that was for sure.

He grabbed a chilled eighteen-pack of bottles out of the refrigerated case and plunked it on the counter. The bored-looking teenager wrestled his eyes off the television in the corner for long enough to ring up the purchase on the register.

What a shit job this must be for a kid his age. Getting minimum wage for the Saturday night shift at a convenience store while all his friends were probably out having fun.

Cooper thanked the good Lord every time something like seeing this kid miserable behind the counter reminded him how good he had it as a professional bull rider.

Getting paid to do what he loved, being famous and having an unending stream of willing pussy—how could a man beat that? He couldn't.

God willing, he'd be able to keep at it for a good long time. He could go to near forty, though that would really be pushing the upper age limits in the sport.

Thoughts of retirement were enough to depress a man, even a world champion like himself. He could have close to ten more years as a pro rider if his body didn't give out on him. No need to spoil a good Saturday night by worrying about something that far into the future.

He paid the kid and shoved his change into his pocket before grabbing the beer off the counter. Ready to be home again, he headed out to the truck.

As he fired up the big diesel engine, he made his game plan. Step one, put the beer in the fridge, minus one for himself. Step two, get out of these boots and jeans so he could be comfortable, kick up his feet on the coffee table and maybe watch a little television.

If the pretty little thing he'd left behind was still awake, he'd maybe have some more fun with her. If not, no big deal. He'd gotten off once already tonight, and there was always the morning.

Yup. It was a damn good life he had.

Cooper tried to remember that when about a mile from the house, the truck's engine went dead silent. With the power steering and power brakes gone, it took both hands and a good amount of strength to steer the heavy vehicle to the side of the road. He had to stand on the brake pedal to bring the two-ton pickup to a stop.

"What the fuck?" There was no one in the truck to respond to his question, but he could venture a guess at the answer himself. Something had to be wrong with the computer controlling the electrical system.

Frigging new vehicles. Everything was high-tech and computerized nowadays. One little faulty computer chip could leave a man stranded and there wasn't a damn thing he could do to fix it.

Give him a good old car or old truck any day. Something from the last century. That he could take apart and put back together again, but not these new pieces of shit.

It was all a moneymaking racket, designed to make a man have to bring it in to the dealer to get serviced rather than handle it himself.

He knew he shouldn't have let Glen talk him into buying this thing. He'd been fine with his old truck. He'd liked that truck. He missed it, especially right now.

Glen had wanted him to buy this piece of crap, so Glen could get his ass dressed and come and get him now.

Trying to find his phone Cooper patted the back pockets in his jeans, then the front breast pocket in his shirt. It wasn't there.

He felt in the console under the dashboard. It wasn't there either.

"Crap." He must not have brought it. How could he not have? He always left it on the front table by the keys.

A memory hit and Cooper got a clear vision of exactly where he'd left his cell—plugged into the wall in the kitchen because the battery had been almost dead.

"Shit." He pounded the dash with the palm of his hand. Hell of a lot of good it would do him there.

Just his luck. Of all the times that phone had been with him and he hadn't needed it, now that he did, it wasn't here.

Maybe whatever was wrong with the truck had been a passing fluke. Taking a shot that his luck had changed, Cooper turned the key in the ignition.

Nothing. Dead silence. The damn engine didn't even turn over. It looked as if he'd be walking the rest of the way home. A mile carrying an eighteen-pack.

On the upside, this could serve as his exercise for the weekend since he hadn't done a hell of a lot much else.

Trying to look on the bright side only pissed him off more, so he grabbed the beer and got out of the truck. After locking the door behind him, he pocketed the keys and let the bad mood consume him with every footstep he took toward home.

Cooper resisted the urge to count each and every step so he could rub it in Glen's face when he finally got there. Glen had talked him into buying the truck. Glen had brought to his attention the fact that they needed beer, and he hadn't offered to get it himself. This was clearly all Glen's fault.

You're making money now, Coop. Why not treat yourself? When could you ever afford a new truck before this? As he put one boot in front of the other, Cooper remembered the truck conversation with Glen clearly.

Bullshit. Two years old and his new truck was breaking down along the side of the highway. His old truck had never left him stranded like this.

Lights coming up from behind him had Cooper turning. Thank God. Maybe whoever it was would give him a ride. He squinted into the glare.

Supporting the weight of the beer in one arm, he stuck his thumb out like a damn hitchhiker and hoped for the best. The car slowed and then pulled onto the shoulder just in front of him.

He jogged to the passenger side. As the window rolled down, he leaned low. "Hey. Thanks for stopping. I broke down. I live just—"

"I know. I saw your truck back there. Get in, Cooper. I'll take you home." The familiarity of her voice jostled his memory, though he was having trouble pinning down who it belonged to.

He reached out, grabbed hold of the handle and opened the door. The overhead dome light illuminated a familiar face that had him smiling. "Hey, funny meeting you here."

"Lucky is more like. You're close to home, but not close enough to be walking. Especially at this time of night. You could get run down being on foot on this dark road."

"You ain't kidding." Cooper slid into the passenger seat and put the beer on the floor between his feet. Slamming the door, he turned toward the woman he knew, but not nearly well enough. "I feel ridiculous saying this, but I don't even know your first name."

She laughed. "That's not really a surprise. Since Skeeter calls me Mom, there's no reason you would know my first name."

"Yeah, and I figured I probably shouldn't call you Mom

too. Now, I could call you Mrs. Anderson—" He cocked a brow and let that suggestion hang in the air, hoping she'd give him an alternative to that formality.

"No." She shook her head. "I haven't felt like Mrs. Anderson for quite a few years now. If it weren't for me wanting to have the same last name as Skeeter, I would have gone back to my maiden name long ago. But anyway, just Hannah is fine."

"Hannah." He rolled the name around on his tongue and in his mind. "That's pretty. I like it."

That wasn't any bullshit either, though he'd been known to throw the shit on occasion. Especially if it got him what he wanted with a woman.

Next to him, she shrugged. As she flipped on her directional signal, she glanced in the rearview mirror before pulling out onto the road. "I guess it's okay. I always wanted something more exotic. My name seems so . . . sensible."

Hannah Anderson might be the most sensible woman he'd ever met. He figured he shouldn't say that, because from what he knew, she lived that way out of necessity, not by choice.

Her husband had abandoned her and her son years ago. Back when the kid was only seven. Skeeter, with the indiscretion of youth, had spilled that tidbit during his first bull-riding lesson with Cooper.

Aside from having never heard her first name until now, Cooper had gotten quite a lot of other information regarding this woman from the boy. He'd let out his mother worked two jobs, a day shift and a night shift, six sometimes seven days a week. Obviously, it was a struggle for her to support the two of them as a single mother.

The kid had also informed Cooper that his mother didn't work Sunday mornings because that's when they went to church. Meanwhile, Coop's biggest concern regarding Sunday was that he couldn't buy beer.

They lived in different worlds, him and her, yet they'd somehow collided thanks to one little boy who wanted to learn to ride bucking bulls.

"So, you on your way home from work?" Cooper eyed her waitress outfit. One of those god-awful, ugly blue-and-white polyester dresses diners made their staff wear for some inexplicable reason. Though even in the unflattering dress, he could see she had some damn nice curves on her.

Her light-brown hair was pulled up in a tight bun at the back of her head, just like it always had been when he'd seen her either dropping off Skeeter or picking him up. That was likely because she'd been coming directly from one of her jobs—the first as a nurse at the hospital and another at the diner. He supposed both occupations required that her hair be kept up and out of the way.

Whatever the reason for it, the style made Cooper want to set her confined tresses free. Watch her hair cascade down her back so he could run his hands through the silky strands. Bury his nose in it and see what she smelled like up close.

"I had the late shift at the diner. Good tips on a Saturday night, so I don't mind too much."

"And Skeeter? Where's he at while you're working?"

"He's home. Hopefully in bed sleeping, though more likely he's up watching television. When his grandfather was alive, they'd be home together while I worked, but my father's no longer with us."

"Yeah. Skeeter mentioned that. I'm sorry for your loss."

"Thank you. Anyway, Skeeter refuses to stay with a sitter anymore. He's eleven now. I was babysitting other people's kids at his age, so I guess I can't argue. And I've known our neighbors forever so he could always go to them if he got scared." She drew in a breath and let it out before continuing. "I suppose compared to letting him ride those damn bulls he loves so much, leaving him home alone for a few hours is nothing."

She sounded weary. It made Cooper want to wrap his arms around her and hug her. The urge was so unlike him that it set his head spinning. But hell, maybe it wasn't such a strange impulse after all, because he wanted to do far more than just hug her. At least that urge was familiar territory.

"Here we are. Home, sweet home." She'd already pulled into his driveway, but until she'd said something, he hadn't realized it. He'd been so enthralled by this woman and the unnecessarily hard life she lived that he hadn't noticed they'd already covered the short distance to his place.

He wanted to say something before he got out and let her drive away. "He's a great kid, Hannah. God knows, I'm no expert, but I think you're doing a really good job with him."

"Thanks." She let out a sigh. "It just doesn't feel like enough. If you didn't let him come here to work and ride, he'd have no man in his life at all. That's no way for a boy to grow up."

Unable to deal with the enormity of the reality that he was the only male influence in this impressionable kid's life, Cooper shook his head. "Having no father in his life is far better than having a bad one. Believe me, I know." He'd learned that from his own childhood.

Still, a question remained. Why this woman was alone was beyond him. Were men nowadays so stupid they couldn't recognize a keeper when they saw one? Cooper could see clearly Hannah was just that, but he wasn't in the market for a wife or a kid.

The outdoor light on his front porch filtered into the car so he could see her as she shook her head. "I just want more for him, you know?"

"You deserve more too. So much more. One day, you're gonna get it." Just because Cooper couldn't have a future with her, didn't mean he shouldn't make her feel better about herself.

She raised her eyes to meet his. "You think so? I'm not so sure."

"I know so." Cooper found himself leaning toward her as she leaned in toward him. When had they gotten so close? He could hear every breath she took even over the sound of the motor running.

"Thanks. I hope you're right." Her gaze dropped to his

lips before she raised it back to his eyes.

Crap. He could think of nothing else but closing that distance and kissing this woman, even though she was the last person on earth he should be kissing. "Hannah."

"Yeah?" She latched onto her lower lip with her teeth.

He tracked the movement with his eyes. "I can't do this."

"Do what?"

He swallowed but his throat still felt dry. "Kiss you."

"But you're not kissing me." Her voice was barely a whisper.

"No, but I want to."

Her eyes narrowed. "And I want you to."

"Christ." Sanity lost, he crashed his mouth against hers.

She responded with an enthusiasm to match his own, reaching up and grabbing the back of his head with both hands. She slid her tongue between his lips and he groaned.

After being with girls who were too young to know what the hell they wanted, it felt good being with a woman who not only knew, but was ready to take, what she needed from him.

Hannah sat facing him in the seat with one knee bent. When Cooper reached out, he connected with the bare skin of her leg.

Her skirt and the position made it too damn easy for him. He slid his hand up the inside of her thigh. She dragged in a ragged breath through her nose. That only encouraged him to go where he knew he shouldn't, all the way to the crotch of her underwear. She responded by leaning in and kissing him harder, tangling her tongue with his.

He rubbed a thumb over her most sensitive spot through the soft cotton and a visible shudder ran through her. Christ almighty, she was responsive. He repeated the action, and Hannah rewarded him with a tiny sound so raw and full of need it sent a shiver down his spine.

What he could do with some time, a little more space and her naked. Or hell, even if he just slid that finger beneath those underwear and into her.

What would she do when he spread her wide and worked her in earnest?

His mind boggled at the thought—before the image of Skeeter's goofy grin careened into his brain.

Cooper remembered how excited the kid had been when he'd agreed to take him on for lessons. How Skeeter had run to tell his mother, smiling from ear to ear. How concerned she'd looked when she'd no doubt began to calculate the many costs of having a son who wanted to learn to be a bull rider.

What kind of a man was he, taking advantage of a woman like Hannah?

The girl he'd picked up at the bar was inside, and he was just yards away with his hand up the dress of the mother of one of his students.

He was one sick motherfucker.

The accuracy of that particular term in this situation would have made him laugh, if he hadn't been so disgusted with himself.

Cooper pulled his hand away and broke the kiss. "Hannah, I can't do this."

"I know. I'm not the kind of woman you're used to. I'm not all doe-eyed and just out of school. I don't own pretty clothes. I'm just plain and old and tired." Pulling away, she dropped her arms from around his neck and let out a breath. "It's okay. I understand. You're not interested."

"You shut the hell up." He grabbed her face in his hands to force her to look at him. "You're not any of that. You're amazing. Any man would respect and admire you. Any woman should want to be like you." Cooper dropped his hold on her. "And that's why you need to steer as far away from me as you can. You deserve a man far better than me, Hannah. You and Skeeter both."

"What do you mean?" A crease marred her brow as she shook her head. "Cooper, you're the best man I know."

"No, I'm not." He let out a snort. How could she be so grounded in some respects and so naïve in others?

"You are. You took on teaching my son for free when you knew I couldn't afford to pay you."

He waved her gratitude away. "So what? That's nothing but some time I would have wasted doing something else otherwise."

"It's not nothing. It's absolutely everything to Skeeter."

Cooper was in no position to be everything to anyone. Not to the kid or to her. "Let me tell you about me. I'm drunk most days. I spend far too much money. I don't give a shit about anybody but myself and I'll fuck any woman who'll spread her legs for me."

He'd been deliberately harsh. He had to be, because she was looking at him with hero worship he didn't deserve and wasn't sure he could resist.

Hannah shook her head. "Even if that's all true, I don't care about any of it."

He let out a bitter laugh. "You should care."

"Maybe I'm tired of doing what I should." Her tone told him he could have her right here, right now, if he wanted.

This woman had been so trodden upon by life, and probably by Skeeter's father too, that Cooper could unzip his jeans, shove those plain cotton drawers of hers to one side and plunge into her, no questions asked.

It would be very tempting to do exactly that. But for once in his life, he was going to do the right thing.

Unlike the girl inside, who he had no intention of ever running across again, Hannah was someone he'd have to see. Soon too. The next time this sweet, hardworking, caring woman brought her son around.

Cooper knew exactly where his soul would be going when the time came to put him in the ground, and it wasn't where this woman would end up when her time came. He wouldn't be the one to tarnish her goodness.

"Go home, Hannah. It's late." He opened the door, grabbed the bag with the beer inside from the floorboard and climbed out of the car. "Thanks for the ride."

"Wait. Should I still bring Skeeter over to work next week

"... or not?" Her question, as well as the hesitation he heard in it, stopped Cooper dead in his tracks.

When he turned back, he saw the uncertainty in her expression. All it did was make him angry. At her for not being stronger and threatening to kick his ass if he did back out of their deal over something like this. At himself for acting like a horny prick with his hand up her skirt in the front seat of her car.

"Of course, you bring him. Dammit, Hannah, don't you see? Skeeter's what's keeping me from burying myself in you so deep neither one of us would come up for air for hours. Yes, I'll still work with him, I'll teach him, but you need a good man to be a father to him and a husband to you. That man sure as fuck ain't me." Cooper remembered the other thing that had yanked him away from Hannah's tempting lips. "Now, 'scuse me. I need to get back inside because there's a girl I barely know waiting on me to fuck her. And I'm gonna, then say goodbye and hope I never see her again. That's the kind of guy I am, Hannah. You need to remember that."

She pursed her lips and shook her head. "No. That's the kind you think you are, but you're not. Not really."

Cooper let out a breath. "Woman, you need to believe a man when he tells you the truth."

"When you do, I will."

Now she decided to grow a backbone. Shaking his head, Cooper slammed the door of the car and took a step back.

God help Hannah and her misplaced blind faith. It was bound to get her hurt. The one thing he could take solace in was that he'd come to his senses in time. He wouldn't be the one to hurt her.

He turned and headed for the house, afraid if he waited and watched her drive away, he'd regret his decision. Bad enough that he regretted not being the kind of man she needed in her life, because damn, he'd sure enjoy having her in his for a little while.

Laurie, or Lauralee, or whatever the hell her name was, was sound asleep on the sofa when he walked through the living room. He continued on to the kitchen and slid the beer onto the shelf of the fridge before he went back out to her.

She could sleep more later. Right now, he was frustrated and hard as a rock after the encounter in the car with Hannah.

"Wake up, darlin'. Time for bed." He nudged her foot with the toe of his boot.

"Mmm?" She wrinkled her nose and cracked her eyes open. "What time is it?"

"Time to get out of those clothes and underneath me, that's what time it is. I've got a hankering for some of that sweet loving of yours." He bent down and flung the girl over his shoulder.

Yup, just as he'd figured. She didn't weigh a whole lot more than a sack of feed.

She squealed as he carried her toward his room. He only hoped she fucked as well as she sucked, because he had a pretty big need to slake, and she was the only one who was around to handle it.

He was in the mood for some good hard pounding. Maybe that would drive the memory of Hannah's sweet kisses out of his head.

Hannah. The one woman on earth he'd never be able to have. Of course, that made her the one woman he wanted.

He was sure fucked up, but he was too damn old to go changing now.

CHAPTER TWO

"Mom, what took you so long? I have to get to Cooper's or he'll have done all the afternoon chores before I get there."

"What took me so long?" Hannah leveled her gaze at her son. "Hmm, well, let's see. I had to go home, change from my scrubs into my waitress uniform, make you a sandwich for your dinner and drive here."

She didn't mention she'd taken the time to fix her makeup as well. She'd done that each and every time she'd dropped off or picked up Skeeter over the past two weeks.

Why she bothered, she didn't know.

Hannah envisioned Cooper, grocery-store bag in hand, heading toward his house and the pretty young thing he said had been waiting for him in his bed . . . all after he'd kissed Hannah silly, woken parts of her she'd have rather left sleeping, and then rejected her.

Crazy. A woman her age, a mother of an eleven-year-old, should know better. Yet she still glanced at her reflection in the rearview mirror to make sure she looked okay while Skeeter tossed his school bag into the backseat and reached for the seat belt.

Once her son was safely buckled in, Hannah threw the car into gear.

She felt that all too familiar flutter in her belly as she turned out of the school lot and headed toward Cooper's place. How long was that going to happen before her body finally got the message her mind knew so well—Cooper wasn't interested in her that way. If he had been, he wouldn't have walked away from her that night, no matter what.

The ranch came into view and the beating of Hannah's heart picked up speed. It was all she could do not to press harder on the accelerator to reach her destination faster.

That would have been fine with Skeeter. He looked ready to leap from the car before she even came to a stop.

She parked between the house and the barn, disappointed to see Cooper wasn't outside or anywhere in view.

"Thanks, Mom." Skeeter swung the passenger door wide.

"Wait. You forgot your sandwich."

"Aw, Mom. I'm not hungry." It seemed eleven-year-old boys had whining down pat.

"You will be before I come pick you up after I'm done with the dinner shift."

"Listen to your mother, kid." Cooper's deep voice had Hannah's heart clenching.

She hadn't heard him walking up to the driver's window since all her attention had been on Skeeter as he tried to escape out the passenger door without taking his dinner.

"Grab your sandwich and go put it in the kitchen fridge," he continued, unaware of how just hearing his voice sent a shiver through her. "We'll get the chores done and then we'll break for some eats."

"You think I can get on some bulls today?" Skeeter asked Cooper over the roof of the car.

"Yeah, you can get on some bulls, if you do everything I tell you, like eating the sandwich your mother went to the trouble of making you." The tenor of his voice shot straight to Hannah's core, making her insides clench with need.

It heated her in spite of the amusement she heard in his

tone at her son's question.

"Yes, sir." Skeeter leaned in the open car door. "Where is it, Mom?"

Trying not to feel bad that her own son did what Cooper asked without question while all he did was argue with her, she lifted the brown paper bag from between the seats. He grabbed it and slammed the car door with a quick thanks and sprinted for the house.

Swallowing hard from the nerves that had her pulse racing whenever she was near this man, Hannah turned in her seat to face Cooper as he stood next to the car, looking as good as ever.

He was all long legs and hard muscles and she couldn't help but imagine running her hands—or her tongue—over every inch of him. She realized she probably should say something or else run the risk that he might leave.

She wanted nothing more than for him to stay, even if all she could do was look at him. "Thanks for that."

"For what?" He cocked a brow above those golden-brown eyes flecked with green. Eyes she could stare into for hours and never get bored of . . . especially if he was braced over her in bed at the time.

It was images such as those that had her throat closing, making it hard to speak or even think around him.

"For keeping him in line. I could have talked until I was blue in the face and he wouldn't have listened. Meanwhile, one word from you and he does whatever you say." Talking about Skeeter with Cooper helped wrest her mind back from her pointless romantic fantasies about this man.

"Eh, he listens to me because I have something he wants. He knows if he doesn't do what I say, he doesn't get on any bulls later." His crooked grin tipped up one corner of his mouth, drawing her attention to his lips and the memories of that kiss.

Cooper had something Hannah wanted too, but it had nothing to do with his animals.

She forced her gaze up to his eyes, in shadow beneath the

brim of his cowboy hat. "Maybe I should get a bucking bull or two of my own. Keep 'em over at my place to use as leverage over my son when he won't eat his broccoli."

He laughed, the action reaching all the way to his eyes as they crinkled in the corners. "That I'd like to see."

If Cooper would come over and help her tend the animals, she might consider it—if she had more than a postage-stamp-sized yard. The lawn at her house couldn't sustain any animal much larger than a cat or maybe a small dog. Definitely nothing of the bovine variety.

"Thanks for taking him today." She didn't want to leave. How long could she keep making small talk just so she didn't have to part with this man? How long before he saw her for what she really was—a silly woman with a huge schoolgirl crush?

He dipped his head. "My pleasure. As always. Heading to work now?" His focus dropped to her uniform.

Remembering the feel of his hand on her bare skin that night, if only for a short while, had Hannah glancing down at her required work wear and wishing it was more flattering. "Yeah. Dinner shift at the diner, but I don't have to close so I can leave right after the rush. I should be able to get here to pick him up a little after seven, maybe seven thirty. Is that too late?"

"It's fine."

"Okay. Good. Thanks." God almighty, she needed to work on her flirting skills. Though in her own defense, she had sat in this very seat a couple of short weeks ago and kissed Cooper. That she was still able to speak to him at all was pretty amazing. "Um, so I'll see you later then."

"Yes, ma'am." He tipped his hat. "Have a good night, Hannah."

"Thanks. You too."

It wasn't until he stepped around the car and headed up the stairs to the porch of the house that she felt she could breathe again.

She backed the car up and maneuvered around so she

could pull out of the drive. A four-hour shift at the diner and then she'd be back here, holding her breath and hoping to see him again. Only then, her less-than-attractive uniform would be stained and she'd smell like food. She let out a sigh.

Her only hope was that the scent of greasy fries acted as an aphrodisiac on him. Otherwise, the possibility of her attracting Cooper Holbrook looked pretty bleak.

~ * ~

A few hours later, Cooper reached into the fridge and grabbed a cold bottle of beer. The kid's mother would be there to get him soon. He didn't see any reason why he couldn't kick back with a brew now that his workday was done.

The stock was all fed and watered and so was the kid. Skeeter was eating his sandwich and drinking his sweet tea. He'd insisted on riding before he'd eat, so it was late for dinner, but better late than never, he figured.

Time to relax and wind down. Cooper pried the cap off his bottle and tossed the opener onto the counter. He leaned back against the edge of the sink and took a sip. As the cold liquid slid down his throat, chasing away the dryness, he watched the kid dig into the sandwich his mama had made him.

Skeeter was like a ball of contained energy. He vibrated with it, even after chores, a hard workout on the bucking barrel and then a few buck-offs in the practice ring that had knocked the wind right out of him.

A man had to appreciate a boy like that. Cooper decided to tell him so. "You did good today, kid."

His wide-eyed gaze whipped up. "Really?"

"Yeah, really." Cooper smiled and then took another pull from the bottle. "Hey, so I was thinking. There's this competition coming up. It's a pro rodeo I'm riding in not far from here—"

"Can I come and watch you ride?"

"Yeah, you can come and watch, but if you'd let me finish, I was gonna say there's a junior division—"

Skeeter's eyes widened. "Can I enter? How old do I have to be?"

If this kid would let Cooper complete a sentence, he'd have all the answers he wanted.

"As I was saying." Cooper raised a brow and waited a beat. When the boy didn't interrupt him again, he continued, "The juniors ride before the main competition starts. You're old enough to compete—"

The boy's mouth opened, as if he was about to launch into more questions. Cooper held up his hand to stop him. Skeeter clamped his mouth shut, drawing his lips in like he was trying to lock them to keep from talking.

Cooper had to smile at the effort as he went on, "But you need your mom to sign the waiver and you need to pay the entry fee."

"How much is it?" That question was asked with far less enthusiasm than the others had been.

He had his suspicions, but Cooper had to wonder exactly how tight the finances were at the Anderson household. "Forty dollars."

Skeeter's relief was visible. "Okay. I can pay that. I've been saving my money from cutting lawns."

"A'ight. Sounds like a plan." Cooper nodded. "You can come in the truck with me if your mom is working. I'm riding, so I'll be going anyway."

"Wait." It was as if a light bulb went off in the kid's head. His eyes opened wide. "You're riding there too?"

"Yup." Cooper cocked a brow. "That's what I told you before, while you were too busy asking all your questions to really listen to me."

Skeeter drew in a breath so big it visibly expanded his chest inside his T-shirt. "I'd be riding in the same competition that you are?"

Cooper let out a laugh as the kid's eyes got comically wide and it looked as if his eyeballs were in danger of popping out and rolling across the floor. "We'll be riding at the same event, yes, but it's not the same competition. The junior division will be scored separately."

"But we'll be riding in the same arena on the same day?"

"Yeah, we will." Cooper nodded.

The kid's face grew impossibly brighter at that information. "I can't wait to tell Mom. And the guys at school."

Smiling, Cooper shook his head, amazed at how it didn't take all that much to make this kid happy. Hell, more than happy. Ecstatic. He was grinning so wide he could barely eat his sandwich. It warmed Cooper's heart to know he had even a small part in that.

"So what day is it? The competition, I mean," Skeeter asked.

"Next Sunday afternoon."

"Sunday!" The kid's excitement reached another level. "Mom usually doesn't have to work on Sundays. Only once in a while at the hospital, but she worked last weekend so that means she won't have to work this weekend. She'll be able to come and see me."

"Yeah. She'll love that, I'm sure." Luckily, the kid didn't pick up on the sarcasm in Cooper's tone.

The image of Skeeter flat on his back in the arena today, gasping for breath after a hard fall, came to mind. That had been the ride after he'd wind-milled off the back of another bull and landed face down and sputtering in the dirt.

The kid was fine, of course. That he was sitting there devouring a sandwich while chattering was proof of that, but Cooper was sure no mother could watch her son in the arena without feeling every hit herself.

For his age and level of experience, Skeeter was good. He was a natural. Cooper and Glen had both said it and meant it. That he was good was no bullshit, but injuries happened.

While riding bulls, it wasn't a matter of if, but rather a question of when the kid would get hurt. Cooper wasn't sure Hannah would be able to handle seeing Skeeter hurt, or hell, even be able to watch him have a bad buck-off.

Nurse or not, Hannah treating injured strangers at the

hospital would be a very different experience from witnessing her son get hurt.

That was one thing his own mother had never had to deal with—watching him wreck live in the arena. Cooper's mother had never seen him ride that he knew of, unless she watched him on television. He wouldn't know if she did or not, not having seen or talked to her since she'd left.

He'd been just about Skeeter's age at the time.

What kind of mother walked out on her kid, even if things were bad?

A sound outside drew his attention. The car pulling into the gravel drive was a welcome interruption to Cooper's train of thought. Some memories were better off left buried.

"It sounds like your mother's here. Finish up your—"

Skeeter jumped up from his seat and streaked out the doorway, leaving the remains of the sandwich behind and Cooper knew he'd lost him. There'd be no more eating. The kid was too excited.

By the time Cooper deposited his beer on the counter and reached the front porch, Skeeter was already leaning into his mother's window and talking her ear off.

He grinned. The kid had obviously been so anxious to tell her his news he couldn't even wait to get into the car.

As he ambled closer, Cooper caught the concerned expression on her face and realized he'd most likely fucked up. He should have discussed the competition with her first. Gotten her permission before he got the kid all excited about the idea.

Crap. Dealing with kids was unknown territory for him, riddled with minefields Cooper hadn't considered.

He strode down the stairs toward the car. He'd better fix this between the kid and his mother. "Hey, kid. Go on inside and finish eating."

The boy looked at him with big warm golden brown eyes so like his mother's there was no missing the family resemblance. "But I'm done eating."

"No, you're not, but after you are, make sure to put your

plate and glass in the sink. Take your time about it all too. I'm gonna stay here and talk to your mother about some things. Okay?"

"Okay." Skeeter scowled a bit but nodded.

Even as the kid slunk back to the house, Cooper knew he only had a minute to talk to Hannah before he'd be back. "Hey."

"Hi." The concern was clear as she raised her gaze to meet his.

"About this event." He cringed. "Sorry, I didn't ask you first."

"Are you sure he's ready for this? I mean a pro event?"

"He's ready. And it's only a junior event going off before the pro event. The stock manager uses much smaller animals for the kids. The bigger, ranker bulls don't come out until later on for the adult competition."

The crease remained between her brows as she continued to look up at him. "He's only eleven."

"I know, but I was competing at his age." He lifted one shoulder. "I'm still here to tell about it."

"I guess I'm going to have to let him compete sometime." Hannah pressed her hand to her belly, as if holding down the butterflies there.

Cooper leaned down and braced his forearms on the open window. "The first time's the hardest."

"So it'll get easier?" She held his gaze.

"Nope, probably not." He grinned. "Just a little less hard."

She smiled, a small, sad expression. "All right. I trust you. He can ride."

Part of Cooper was thrilled to hear she trusted him, even as a part of him felt genuine fear he wouldn't be able to live up to the trust she'd placed in him. "He'll be real happy about that."

"At least one of us will be." She cocked a brow.

"Hannah, I'll make sure he's a'ight." What was it about this woman that had Cooper making promises he wasn't sure he could keep?

She nodded as Skeeter came barreling out of the house. He pinned Cooper with his stare. "Did she say yes?"

The damn kid had known Cooper was outside trying to talk his mother into letting him compete. That was probably the only thing that had kept him in the house for even the couple of minutes Cooper had gotten alone with Hannah.

He realized Skeeter was far more intuitive than he'd given him credit for. "Yeah, she said yes."

The kid let out a whoop, grinning ear to ear. "Thanks, Mom."

Hannah shook her head. "Thank Cooper. He convinced me you could do this."

Skeeter grinned wider. "Thanks, Cooper."

"You're welcome. Now, get in the car. Your mother's had a long day. I'm sure she wants to get home."

As the kid flung the passenger door wide and scrambled into the seat, Cooper moved back from the car. "Have a good night, Hannah."

"Thanks. You too."

There was a weird dynamic between him and her. There had been since that night he'd screwed up and let himself kiss her.

On the surface, the common ground between them was Skeeter. Cooper had willingly put himself in that position by offering to be his teacher, which had also turned into him being the sole male influence in the kid's life. That was fine. He could handle that. He was a mentor to the younger riders on the tour too.

It was this other thing—the attraction simmering between him and Hannah just below the surface—that he hadn't signed up for. That was something he couldn't give in to.

He turned toward the house, climbed the stairs but didn't go inside. Instead, he leaned against the rail of the porch and watched the glow of the taillights as her car pulled to the end of the driveway. Even as the late summer sun set and the darkness began to creep in and overtake the daylight, he could see Skeeter.

The kid leaned out the passenger window and waved, shouting, "See you this weekend."

Cooper lifted one arm and nodded.

Glen walked up and leaned next to him. "She likes you."

"Who?" He had a feeling he knew the answer to that question already. Glen knew him too damn well for his liking.

"The mother."

"Yeah, so? Everyone likes me. I'm a likeable guy."

"Yeah, yeah. You know what I mean." Now that the car was out of view, Glen turned. Pinning Cooper with his gaze, he leaned his ass on the rail and crossed his arms. "So why don't you ask her out?"

"Because that piece of tail comes with a kid I have to teach every week."

Glen frowned. "You're a dick. I didn't say screw her for a night and then never talk to her again, the way you usually do with women. I said ask her out. Like on a date. You do remember what a date is, don't you? You eat. You talk. You get to know each other. You actually remember each other's names . . ."

Cooper lifted one brow. "Sounds like a lot of work for a little pussy."

The sound Glen let out, accompanied by his scowl, told Cooper exactly how he felt about that statement.

"I'm going inside for a beer." As Glen stomped across the porch and into the house, Cooper noticed his partner hadn't offered to get him one.

Fine. He'd get his own damn beer. It would be easier than bowing to the pressure of Glen's matchmaking.

Truth be told, Cooper wouldn't mind going through all of that dating bullshit Glen had talked about with Hannah, but that wasn't meant to be. Cooper wasn't in the market for a wife or a son. Hannah and Skeeter deserved a man who was.

Best friend or not, Cooper wasn't going to get into talking with Glen about Hannah and all his feelings about her and the situation. Best to let sleeping dogs lie. He'd fucked up once by kissing her, but he wouldn't do that again. Even if seeing her just now had caused a bone-deep awareness of his attraction to her—both mentally and physically.

That he genuinely liked her as a person he could handle—but not at the same time as this balls-deep ache that wanting her caused. That he'd have to deal with on his own.

On top of this thing with Hannah, a restlessness was starting to creep up on him. It happened whenever he wasn't out on the road riding the circuit. This break between the bigger competitions was only a few weeks long, but it felt like an eternity. The itch to get out and do something—or someone—was hitting Cooper especially hard after seeing Hannah.

He pushed through the front door. "Wanna go out for a beer instead?" Cooper needed to hit up a bar, grab a girl and get busy. Then he'd feel better.

Glen shook his head as he reached into the fridge for a bottle. "Nah, I wanna stay home tonight. I'm tired."

"Tired?" He let out a snort at the ridiculousness of that. "Come on. You can sleep when you're dead."

"You don't have to stay home on account of me." Glen popped the top off the longneck. "You go if you want to."

"It's not as much fun alone." Cooper screwed up his mouth. Glen was acting like an old man.

"I'm sorry that I'm not up to entertaining you." Glen rolled his eyes before taking a pull out of the bottle.

"So am I." Cooper headed for the fridge and a beer when what he really wanted was a girl and to fuck. That gave him an idea. Why go out when you could stay in? He followed Glen into the living room. "Hey, you get the number of that girl you were with when we had them here a couple of weeks ago? You remember. The night the piece of shit new truck you talked me into buying broke down."

"Yeah, yeah. I remember. And your damn truck is fixed now, so shut the hell up about that already." Glen kicked his feet up on the coffee table and reached for the television remote. "And yeah, I got her number. Why?"

"Give her a call. See if she and her friend wanna come

over tonight."

Glen raised his brows. "You never do repeats."

"Maybe I'm changing." That was a lie.

The truth was, Cooper needed to do something about this itch or the next time sweet Hannah Anderson bit her lip and raised those deep-chocolate eyes to him, he'd have her on her back on the hood of her car. He'd slide inside and not give a shit about the rights or wrongs of the situation.

"Or maybe you're just horny." Glen shot Cooper a glance and then focused back on the television.

"That too." Cooper lifted one shoulder in a shrug. No use denying it.

"A'ight. I'll call her." Glen tossed the remote on the table and reached into his pocket for his cell phone.

"Good."

Cooper and Glen had been buddies for years. They did most things together, especially now they were partners in the ranch. Glen took care of things while Cooper traveled to compete. But even as close as they were, Cooper still felt more comfortable keeping things, such as feelings when he had them, to himself.

Maybe it was the result of his crap childhood. Or maybe he was just an antisocial son of a bitch at heart. Either way, he wouldn't admit to Glen what a temptation Hannah's kisses had been.

Cooper would, however, admit to his friend he was horny as hell. That need, any man could understand. No emotions necessary, just the way he liked it.

After some talk, most of which Cooper didn't bother listening to, Glen disconnected the call.

Cooper raised a brow. "Well?"

"She's coming."

"And her friend?" Whatever her name was.

"She thinks her friend's free tonight. She's calling her to make sure, then she'll pick her up on the way over here."

"A'ight. Good." Finally, something was going his way. With satisfaction on the horizon, Cooper walked to the kitchen.

He didn't need another beer, his was still full, but he needed to move. He opened cabinets and closed them again, and then pulled open the door on the fridge and stared at the contents for a bit. He wandered back to the living room and plopped down on the sofa.

Cooper tried sitting next to Glen and watching TV, but he was too restless. After a little bit, he got up one more time and headed into the kitchen again.

"What the devil are you looking for in there?" Glen called from the other room.

"Damned if I know." With a sigh, Cooper slammed shut the door of the cabinet he'd just opened.

Something to occupy his mind, most likely. Sad to say, he doubted the girl on their way there now would do it, but it was worth a try. She'd occupy his hands and his cock, but his mind—doubtful.

"You riding this weekend?" Glen shot him a sideways glance when Cooper strolled back to the living room doorway and hovered there.

"Yeah. Local event." He didn't sit. He moved to the window, wondering when the girls would arrive.

"Thank God for that." The relief was clear in Glen's tone.

Cooper couldn't agree with him more. It seemed only strapping his hand to a bucking bull in front of a roaring crowd would calm the restlessness. Even sinking into a woman wouldn't help for long.

God help them all when the time came for him to retire. On that depressing thought, he heard the crunching of tires as a car pulled into the driveway. One glance out the window confirmed it.

He donned a smile. "Girls are here."

Glen planted his booted feet on the floor and stood. "Well, thank God for that too.

CHAPTER THREE

Cooper ignored that he felt Hannah's gaze on him, watching every move he made behind the chutes as he helped her kid get ready to ride.

He reminded himself she was there for Skeeter. She was looking this way, her stare pinned to the action on top of the chute because she was watching her son, not him as he tried to help the kid.

She was scared. He could see that clearly as she held the top rail of the fence with a white-knuckled grip. He wanted to go to her. Tell her the kid would be fine. That Skeeter was ready for this.

He wanted to be with her during the ride too. Put his arm around her and calm the nerves he knew he'd feel making her body tremble.

The thought of Hannah shaking beneath his hands had him thinking about sex. Christ, he was a sick man.

Cooper forced his attention back where it needed to be—on Skeeter. He might not actually get paid for their lessons, but he was still the kid's teacher, and the boy needed his guidance now.

Riding one of the bulls in the practice ring at the ranch

was one thing. Climbing into the chute for his first public competition was a whole other level of nerve-wracking.

Cooper knew the adrenaline would be pumping through the kid like an illicit drug. A veteran rider could use the hormone flooding his bloodstream right before a ride to help him focus. In a newbie like Skeeter, that surge could just as easily lead to poor decisions and stupid mistakes, and ultimately, an injury.

"You ready, kid?" Cooper glanced down at his protégé, inspecting him to see for himself that the boy's equipment was on properly.

His helmet already strapped beneath his chin, Skeeter nodded.

"Spurs on, good and tight. Chap straps buckled. Safety vest zipped. Glove on and taped." Working from the feet up, Cooper ran through the pre-ride checklist aloud for the kid's benefit. He reached Skeeter's head in his list and asked, "Mouth guard in?"

"Yes, sir." The response was mumbled and barely audible, proving Skeeter was indeed speaking through the piece of plastic.

Cooper had already supervised Skeeter cleaning and rosining his bull rope when they'd arrived, so he knew that was good to go. The stock handler was looping the rope beneath the bull that was in the chute now.

Ready or not, it was time. But the kid was ready. Cooper felt it with certainty. Not all eleven-year-olds could handle strapping themselves to the back of a bucking bull in front of a crowd.

Skeeter was not most kids.

He was a natural, though Cooper tried not to tell him that too often. Gifted with God-given talent or not, rising to be the best in this business took hard work and dedication.

That was something Cooper feared he'd begun to forget lately. At the very least, he'd let it slip a bit. There was never a time to be complacent. To rest on the laurels of past successes.

The problem was it was easy to do when time and time again he'd gotten away with it. On too many occasions, he'd spent the night drunk in some stranger's bed and then had woken up hurting and still gone on to win the event.

Winning was as addictive as the adrenaline rush of riding. Both acted upon him like a drug.

Continuing to win, even after doing what he knew was bad for him and his career, was as dangerous as any drug out there. As long as it kept happening, he didn't see compelling motivation to make a change coming anytime soon.

Now was not the time or place for introspection. He was there to put Skeeter on the proper path to becoming a champion. The straight and narrow road Cooper had strayed from.

Skeeter idolized him, so it was doubly important that the crooked line his own life had taken not serve as an example for this kid.

It might be too late for him, but if nothing else, he could point Skeeter in the right direction. "You're ready for this, kid. Get on up there and take your wrap."

After a nod, the boy climbed up to the top rail. Before he lowered himself into the chute, he glanced up and scanned the crowd.

Cooper knew who he was looking for. "Your mom's here, kid. She's watching. Don't you worry about that. Concentrate on the ride. She'll be waiting for you when you get done."

Skeeter glanced back at Cooper and nodded one more time before lowering himself onto the back of the bull.

He hadn't lied to Hannah when he'd told her the bulls would be appropriate to the level of skill in the junior division. The one that Skeeter had gotten in the draw was small. It had to be. The rules specified no animal could weigh more than 750 pounds in the nine to twelve-year-old boys division.

Skeeter had ridden bigger animals at Cooper's place. He could handle this one.

After being a bit jumpy when it had first run into the

chute, the bull stood calmly now even as Cooper balanced his boot heels on the rails and reached to grab the end of Skeeter's rope. He used both hands to pull the rope tight before handing it off to Skeeter.

It wasn't lost on Cooper that in his lifetime he'd ridden at some of the biggest and most famous arenas and events in the world. Las Vegas. Calgary. Madison Square Garden. Yet there he was feeling a little nervous while pulling the rope for a boy in the junior division of a local event in Arkansas.

The strangest part was Cooper felt really good. It was as if he was doing something important. Something that mattered.

Skeeter wrapped the rope around his gloved hand, laid it across his palm before closing his fingers and pounding his fist like Cooper had shown him. It was a textbook wrap.

Glancing down, he made sure the kid's feet were in proper position. His heels were in, his toes out and his spurs were clear of the rope—proof the kid did listen when Cooper talked, even if most days he seemed to bounce off the rails with excitement over getting to ride.

Cooper caught Skeeter's attention. "Whenever you're ready, you give the gateman a nod."

The kid pounded his closed fist one more time and then wiggled his ass on the back of the bull as if checking that he was centered.

When he finally nodded, it was accompanied by a muffled, "Go!"

The gateman swung the gate wide. On that cue, the bull dug his hooves into the soft dirt and rocketed into the arena.

The damn animal had gone from docile to powerhouse in a matter of seconds, but Skeeter maintained his center even through the force of the changes.

For being small and lean, the animal was a good, strong bucker. If Skeeter could hang on to his rope for the eight seconds and not get fouled for a slap, he could get a damn good score.

It was a nearly perfect ride. The kid broke at the hips, absorbing the energy of every leap the animal made. The bull started out spinning into Skeeter's riding hand only to reverse to spin against it, but the kid made the adjustment and hung on.

The buzzer sounded and Skeeter reached down with his free arm, yanked the tail of his bull rope and released his wrap.

Throwing his leg over the bull's head and jumping off on the outside of the spin, he made a perfect dismount, even landing on his feet. Cooper finally let himself breathe after holding his breath for the duration of the ride.

"Holy shit, that kid can ride. He yours?" The voice next to Cooper had him turning.

"Yeah." Cooper nodded to the man and then realized that had sounded wrong. "I mean, I taught him. He's my student but nah, he's not my kid."

"Well, you did a damn good job teaching him."

"I wish I could take the credit, but honestly, not much of it was my doing. Damn kid's a natural." Cooper shot the guy a look. "Don't tell him I said that. Don't want him getting too big for his britches."

The stranger laughed. "Gotcha."

For a few seconds, Cooper felt emotions swirling inside him—a strange mix of the warmth of pride mingled with a cold, hollow emptiness and regret he didn't have a son of his own to teach. His own boy he could take credit for and feel this overwhelming pride over. But that's all the feeling lasted—a few seconds.

The reality was he had one great fucking life just the way it was. He could do what he wanted. Who he wanted. When he wanted.

He held on tight to that thought as he watched Skeeter come out of the arena, dusty and grinning, and his mother ran to greet him.

They'd likely go out for ice cream or some such family thing after this to celebrate. And after his own event, Cooper would celebrate himself. With any luck, he'd sweet-talk that young thing who'd been eyeing him from the bleachers into going out to his truck for a quickie.

That's the way life worked for him. If more folks learned what worked best for themselves and stopped trying to have something else, something more, there wouldn't be single mothers raising boys alone. There wouldn't be drunk, angry fathers left with their abandoned sons.

If his parents had done what was best for the family and gotten an amicable divorce back when he was Skeeter's age, he wouldn't have had to listen to his father arguing with his mother after rolling in stinking drunk from a late night out. He wouldn't have heard the slap, or his mother hitting the wall, or the soft sobs she tried to hide after his father finally passed out and they could all breathe freely again that it was over, at least for that night.

And he wouldn't have had to grow up alone with that sullen, angry man after his mother had given up and abandoned them both.

Hell, he'd have been better off if she'd gotten a damn abortion instead of having an unwanted baby and having to marry a man who was wrong for her. There sure as hell had been many times back then that Cooper had wished he'd never been born.

The past needed to stay in the past. He pushed those memories away as Skeeter ran for him, bull rope and cowbell trailing behind him.

The kid grinned from ear to ear. "Did you see me?"

"Of course, I saw you. You did great." Cooper glanced over Skeeter's head as the scoreboard flashed. "Did you see your score?"

Skeeter was used to riding in Cooper's ring, not in front of judges. He'd obviously forgotten there'd be a score involved, and a hell of a score it was too.

"Eighty points, kid. That puts you in the lead."

The boy's eyes widened at that revelation. He turned to his mother and she laughed at the same expression that had Cooper smiling.

Hannah glanced at Cooper. "He must be in shock. I've

never seen him speechless before."

Cooper blew out a loud burst of air. "You ain't kidding. Neither have I."

"I'm in the lead?" Skeeter finally found his voice.

"Yup, but don't get too excited. There are a few more yet to ride."

"I'm gonna go watch." Skeeter spun to his mother. "Can I?"

"Sure. Go ahead." Hannah watched Skeeter run off and let out a breath, holding her hand to her chest. "I thought I'd die watching that. That's it, right? He won't ride again today?"

"He might. If he stays on the leader board, he'll ride in the short go." He noticed the hand she held to her chest trembled and bit back a cuss. "You've never seen him ride, have you?"

Of course, she hadn't. When would she have? The kid only rode at Cooper's place. She'd drop him off and pick him up, but she'd never been there while he'd been in the practice ring.

Thank God, it had been a picture-perfect ride and the kid hadn't wrecked. He hadn't even hit the dirt but had landed dead on his feet like a damn Olympic gymnast or something.

Still, Cooper should have considered Hannah and her feelings about watching her only child in that situation. He should have had her up next to him by the chute so he would be with her for this first time.

This was why he didn't keep women around long enough for them to mean something to him. He was no good at it. They'd only end up getting hurt or scared like Hannah had.

"I'm sorry, Hannah. I should have been there with you for his ride and I wasn't."

"No, you shouldn't have. Skeeter needed you far more than I did. He needed you to pull his rope and make sure he took his wrap properly and check his foot position . . ."

Even as bad as he felt, he let out a laugh at her laundry list of pre-ride tasks. "I see you've gotten the full bull-riding tutorial already."

Hannah rolled her eyes. "You have no idea. There's a running commentary of him explaining things to me every time it's on television. And when you come on screen—well, I'd better not dare breathe too loudly or he might miss something the announcers say about you."

He shook his head but couldn't help his grin as he pictured the scene. "Sorry about that."

She dismissed his concern with a wave. "No problem. I don't mind watching. At least it's one thing we can do together. I can't teach him to ride like you do, but I can sit there with him and watch and make the appropriate comments. Besides, it's more fun watching now that I know the sport better . . . and that I know you."

The damn woman latched her teeth onto her lower lip like he'd seen her do before, and of course, Cooper couldn't help but notice.

He wrestled his focus back to her eyes, but that didn't help because she had that look on her face—hungry yet innocent at the same time. It made him want to lay her on her back with him above her.

Seeing her in real clothes instead of a uniform wasn't helping the situation either. Her jeans hugged her with just the right amount of tightness. Her shirt too. To top it all off, the heel on her cowboy boots accentuated the sexy curve of her ass and the enticing sway of her hips as she walked.

He'd tried not to notice, but hell if he didn't. He needed to knock any ideas about him and Hannah being together that way right out of his head.

"I made Skeeter's favorite dinner for tonight. If you wanted to come over and join us at the house, you're more than welcome. I'm sure he'd love to have you there."

A good meal cooked at home by a beautiful woman was a very tempting offer, which is why Cooper had to say no. "I got something planned for after, but thanks for asking."

"All right. Maybe next time." Hannah nodded.

He tried to ignore the disappointment he imagined he'd heard in her voice, and knew he was lying when he said,

"Sure. Next time."

His gaze cut to where the pretty young thing had been hanging around near the rail watching him. She was still there, but not looking very happy now that Cooper was talking to Hannah. He nearly laughed at that.

Little did the girl know that today was her lucky day. She'd get to add a world champion bull rider to her roster of sexual conquests if she wanted. Cooper would quench his own hunger, while Hannah went home for a nice quiet celebration dinner with her son. Win-win for all of them.

It would be safer that way for everyone involved. That didn't mean Cooper wasn't running that dinner scene in his head. Him, Hannah and the kid, all sitting around a table in a kitchen he imagined being painted a bright, sunny yellow and smelling of the fresh flowers on the table and the hot food on the stove.

Usually when Cooper fantasized about women they were naked. But in this particular daydream, Hannah was in an apron and looking like a happy homemaker from the 1950s. That in itself set off warning bells in his head.

It was even more dangerous than picturing her perched on the edge of that kitchen table while he took her hard and fast to slake this need she caused in him.

"Hey, what is the kid's favorite dinner anyway?" He asked the question to help fill in the details of this extremely ill-advised little fantasy of his.

Yeah, he was a glutton for punishment, but as long as this shit remained in his head and he didn't act on it, he'd be fine.

"Spaghetti and meatballs." She wrinkled her nose and looked adorable while she lifted one shoulder in a half shrug. "Nothing fancy, I know, but it's what he loves best."

He laughed. "That sounds about right. Skeeter does like to stick to the basics. Keep things simple."

So did Cooper. Buckle bunnies and beer. Couldn't go wrong with both of those after a competition was done. Start throwing in things like a woman who probably cooked as good as she looked, and her son who worshipped the ground he walked on and things would no doubt start to get real complicated, real fast.

Cooper didn't like complicated. It was about time he remembered that. With that thought in mind, he tipped his hat to Hannah. "Well, if you'll excuse me. I got somebody I need to talk to."

"Sure." Hannah's sweet smile stuck with him while he walked away.

He imagined he felt her eyes on him as he made a beeline for the girl in the stands. Hannah needed a reality check. This was who he was—a man who enjoyed the moment with no thought for the future. It was about time she saw it for herself and got over that damned hero worship she and her son shared for him.

"Hey, darlin'." He leaned his forearms on the rail when he'd reached his goal—the sweet thing showing more skin than was proper. He saw the girl react when she realized he was talking to her.

She smiled like the devil was inside her and sashayed a few steps closer to him until she was pressed up against the rail. "Hey, yourself."

Cooper wouldn't let himself glance back at Hannah. He knew she'd seen him, just like he knew him walking away from her to flirt with this stranger would cut her deep. But beneath it all was his certainty that sometimes doing the right thing could hurt a person.

In the long run, this right here would save Hannah the whole truckload of pain that falling for him would surely bring her. He wasn't the settling-down kind and his upbringing sure as hell hadn't equipped him to know how to be a father to her kid.

He focused his full attention back to the girl who would hopefully be his future companion for any post-ride activities of the sexual nature. "So, darlin', tell me you have no plans for after the event and you'll make me the happiest man in the world."

If only that were true . . .

~ * ~

"Cooper's up to ride. Watch, Mom, or you'll miss him."

Skeeter needn't have worried. For better or worse, Hannah's gaze had barely left him. She'd watched him strap on the chaps that made him look so damn sexy her palms had started to sweat. She'd seen him clamp his cowboy hat lower onto his head before he climbed into that metal chute that looked too much like a death trap for her liking. And she'd seen the attention the cute young woman in the stands paid to him and the attention he paid her back.

Yup. Hannah hadn't missed any of it, and all it had done was make her more agitated. She hated her attraction to him as much as she hated the knowledge it wasn't reciprocal on his part.

The bull bounced in the chute as Cooper lowered himself onto the beast's back and Hannah hated even more how she worried about his safety when he clearly wasn't hers to worry about.

She laid her hand on Skeeter's shoulder and pulled him closer to her in a hug, grateful he, at least, was done riding for today. "How come Cooper doesn't ride with a helmet like you do?"

"He says it's because he didn't learn to ride with one when he was my age. The weight of it could throw his riding off. But he says it's real important to wear one so that's why he makes me practice with it on, even if we're just on the barrel, so I'm used to it. He says he never wants to hear I've ever ridden without a helmet on or he'll give me a whoopin'." Her son grinned at her. "I don't think he'd really do it though."

The chattering had Hannah smiling even as her heart clenched at hearing how much Cooper worried about her son. How he took care of him for her. "I don't know, sweetie. I wouldn't take a chance if I were you."

No matter what he claimed, Cooper was a better dad to Skeeter than her son's biological father ever had been. It was no wonder she nearly melted whenever Cooper was near. Her poor heart didn't stand a chance . . . and he'd be taking that groupie from the stands home with him by the looks of things.

That alone should squelch her attraction to this man.

It didn't.

The clang of the gate had her gaze snapping to the action in the chute. The bull charged into the arena with the man who so often occupied her thoughts astride its back.

It had been heart-stopping to watch her son strapped by a rope around his hand to the back of a bucking animal, no matter what size it had been. Seeing Cooper in the same position, but on a bull twice as big as the one Skeeter had ridden, was nearly as hard for her to witness.

Watching Cooper on TV in the comfort of her living room was easy compared to this. She'd felt so much more detached before seeing a competition live.

Maybe it was harder to judge size and distance on the small television screen. Here, so close, she could see exactly how tight and confining that chute he crawled into was. Exactly how big and powerful these bulls were. How hard these men hit the ground when they fell. How close those deadly hooves came to striking flesh and bone while the fallen riders lay helpless on the ground.

Just feet away, on the other side of the metal rail that separated the people from the action in the arena, the bull bucked and spun. Cooper matched the moves with countermoves of his own. When the bull dipped forward, the man angled backward. As the animal pushed off the dirt into a high jump, he bent at the hips and absorbed the force of it.

The moves amazed her. It was as if he defied the laws of nature and gravity.

Over the noise of the crowd, Skeeter chief among those cheering, she could hear her pulse pounding in her ears.

It was an amazing dance, the give and take, action and reaction between man and beast. Even more mind-boggling was that the entire thing lasted only eight seconds. Before she knew it, the buzzer sounded and Cooper was reaching down to grab the tail of the rope binding him to the animal.

The bull rope released from around Cooper's gloved hand and he leapt to the ground. He hit his knees but scrambled immediately to his feet and ran for the rail to dodge the bull still in the arena with him.

The bull fighters did their job and distracted the animal while Cooper ran for the perimeter fencing. She hadn't realized she'd been holding her breath until it all came out in one big whoosh when he finally reached safety.

Skeeter spun to face her, grinning wide. "Did you see that? Isn't he amazing?"

She let out a short laugh that her son had voiced the exact thing she'd thought while watching Cooper. "Yeah. He is."

Amazing . . . and not interested in her.

Hannah watched the girl in the stands lean over the rail and wave to get Cooper's attention. Smiling, he exited the arena, bull rope in hand, and moved closer. Acid ate at Hannah's stomach as she watched him bask in the glow of the girl's attention.

"Come on. We have to go congratulate him." Skeeter took a step in Cooper's direction.

"No." Hannah clamped her hand down on her son's shoulder just before he moved out of reach. "Not right now."

He spun back to face her, frowning. "But—"

"Skeeter, give the man some space after his ride. He'll come see us when he's ready."

The scowl told her she'd lost some points with her son over that decree. That couldn't be helped. No more than she could help Cooper's preferences as far as which females he'd rather spend his time with. She was his student's mother and that was all she'd ever be to him.

All the wishing in the world wouldn't change that. It wouldn't make her eighteen again with her tight pre-baby stomach and perky boobs either.

Too bad, since that seemed to be just Cooper's type.

CHAPTER FOUR

A few hours later, Cooper was a little tired, kind of hungry and a bit dustier than he had been at the start of the afternoon, but things were good. He'd scored high and had an envelope filled with that day's first-place winnings stuffed into the back pocket of his jeans—the jeans that hung open and low on his hips.

Grabbing the envelope before it fell out, he shoved it beneath the dashboard so he could better enjoy the girl he'd also scored at the event.

The dim light of dusk covered the action inside the cab of his truck parked on the edge of the lot. He rocked his hips and plunged into that day's conquest beneath him on the bench seat. But in spite of that, rather than lose himself in the moment, he couldn't keep from thinking about how hungry he was.

Starving actually, and dammit, the only thing he could think of was spaghetti and meatballs.

Cooper thrust deep and held there, finishing the perfunctory fuck with a groan. His wandering thoughts hadn't messed with a satisfactory completion to the encounter. He didn't need to concentrate to get off.

Luckily, fucking came as naturally as breathing to him, especially after an event as he rode out the adrenaline highs and lows.

The girl hadn't come, but he wasn't feeling all that bad about it. After he'd worked her with his hand for longer than he usually took to get a woman off, he gave in to his knowledge that not all females were created equal in the orgasm department. He'd tried. What more could he do?

It was getting late and Cooper was tired and hungry and done. Reaching down and feeling around on the floorboards, he found an old fast-food paper bag and ditched the used condom inside.

While fixing his jeans, he wished he could ditch the girl as easily. She smiled up at him now, expectation clear in her eyes.

He hated seeing that expression on a female's face. He could feel the hope radiating off her. She was waiting for him to invite her out, for a meal or a drink. Or maybe she was looking to come back to his place, thinking they'd snuggle all night and wake up in his bed together.

Didn't these women think at all before they offered up their pussy on a silver platter to a total stranger? If a date or a future had been his intention, why the hell would he have fucked her in his truck in the parking lot?

If he'd wanted to take her back to his home, he would have. And before the sex. Not after.

He'd had no intention of her coming back to his place, which is why he'd had to keep his head bent until his neck ached to avoid hitting the cab's ceiling the whole time he'd been screwing her.

It was worth the neck ache though. Always easier to get rid of them at the arena with some bullshit excuse, than it was to get them out of his house later that night or, worst case scenario, the next morning.

"So, you wanna go get a drink or something?" she asked as she straightened her clothes.

"I'd love to, darlin', but I can't. I got someone waiting on me at home. I need to get going." He didn't mention that someone was Glen, who with any luck would have saved him some of whatever he'd cooked for dinner.

That got the expected reaction. Her eyes grew wide before she narrowed them at him. She'd made the assumption he'd hoped, that he had a wife or girlfriend at home. That he was a rotten, cheating bastard.

Good. That meant he wouldn't be seeing this one again. If he did happen to come across her, and if he was inclined toward a repeat, he was sure he could sweet-talk his way around her mad. No problem.

"Can you get back to your car okay?" he asked, giving her one final verbal push out of the truck.

"Yeah. Fine."

It was a dismissal and she knew it. She barely looked at him as she opened the door and slid to the ground.

He called after her, "Have a good night."

Her response was more snort than anything else. He couldn't blame her for being angry. Then again, what did she expect? A ring and a happily ever after for spreading her legs for a man she'd met two hours ago?

Shaking his head at the ridiculousness of it all, he fired up the engine. He waited, watching her get safely into her car and start the engine before he backed out of the space.

Pulling the truck onto the highway and heading toward home felt much too good. Most nights after an event, he'd head for a bar to wind down for a bit. Grab a drink and a bite.

Tonight, he had no desire to go out. He wrote that off to the fact he'd already scratched one itch with the girl. A cold beer and a hot meal he could get, and enjoy better, at home. He didn't need the crowd or noise of a bar for that.

Cooper arrived at the ranch and found Glen in the kitchen. "We got any food? I'm starving."

Glen glanced up from the sink where he looked way too domestic while scrubbing some dishes. It was a good thing at least one of them didn't mind doing shit like washing dirty dishes or this place would be a real pigsty.

"Yeah. There's steak and a baked potato I saved for ya." He tipped his head toward the counter.

Cooper wrinkled his nose at the meat and potato. He'd had spaghetti on his mind all night, but unless he cooked some, that wasn't going to happen. He wandered to the fridge for a beer. At least that was one thing he craved he could have.

"How'd you do?" Glen asked.

"First place." Cooper leaned against the counter. "Now ask me how the kid did."

Glancing over, Glen caught sight of the smug expression on Cooper's face. His eyes widened. "He didn't. Did he?"

Cooper grinned wide. "Yup. First place in the junior bull riding for his age group."

"Hot damn. He must have been bouncing off the rails."

He laughed at the truth of that. "Yeah, pretty much."

That kind of energy and happiness was infectious, and Cooper could use some himself right about now.

Maybe he should have taken the risk. Accepted Hannah's invitation and gone to dinner at their house. The kid would have loved that. Hell, Cooper wouldn't have minded too much either.

By this hour, Skeeter had probably reviewed every second of his winning ride three times over and his poor mother would have had to listen to it each and every time. He knew she would have done it with the same enthusiasm every time too. As if each repetition was the first time. That's the kind of mother Hannah was.

Cooper opened the drawer and grabbed utensils. He took the plate of leftovers from the counter and slid it onto the kitchen table.

He wasn't kidding when he'd told Glen how hungry he was. He hadn't taken time to eat before he rode because he'd been too busy—first with the kid and then with ensuring his after-ride activities with the piece of ass. But instead of picking up his knife and fork and digging in to his dinner now, he pulled his cell phone out of his pocket and hit the number for the kid's house.

"Hello?" Skeeter greeted Cooper, just as he'd braced himself to hear Hannah speaking into his ear.

It was probably better this way. That woman's gentle voice got to him as much as her damn lip biting did.

He let out the breath he'd been holding. "Hey, kid."

"Cooper! I forgot to say before, great ride in the short go."

"Thanks. That's why I called you. To tell you that you did real good today too. I mean that. You made me proud." Cooper couldn't help but notice Glen turn and cock one brow as he listened to the conversation.

"Really? Thanks." Skeeter's excitement was tangible, but Cooper wasn't able to enjoy it with the judgmental expression on the face of the audience of one in attendance.

"You're welcome, kid. So I gotta go, but I'll see you next week. Okay?"

"Okay. See ya."

He disconnected the call and concentrated on the plate in front of him rather than admit he saw the look Glen was still shooting him.

"I thought the reason you didn't want to date the mother was because of the kid." It appeared even Cooper ignoring him didn't prevent Glen from commenting.

Cooper shook his head. "Never said that."

If he remembered correctly, he'd told Glen he didn't want to fuck Hannah because of the kid. He didn't want to date anyone at all. Those were two different things entirely.

The guy should keep his facts straight if he was going to stick his nose in things that were none of his business.

Nothing Glen said mattered anyway. He'd seen Hannah's face today when she saw him with the girl. It was right after the end of the event. Skeeter had dragged her to say goodbye to him. She'd gotten an eyeful of Cooper with his arm around the girl from the stands. He could tell by her expression it had bothered her. Whether that was because she didn't approve or was envious it wasn't her, he didn't know.

Probably a bit of both. He knew women and he knew Hannah. She was interested in him, but he also could assume a good bit about her values. Enough to think that him hooking up with a scantily clad female who was probably ten years his junior wouldn't sit well with her.

Either way, the intentional move had served its purpose. After the display he'd put on for her today, Hannah would never go out—or do anything else—with him even if he did break down during a moment of weakness and ask her. That was definitely for the best for all of them.

"You care about that kid." Obviously, Glen wasn't letting this drop.

"Yeah. So? I care about that damn stray dog you found on the highway and made us take in too. Doesn't mean I have to take in the mutt's mother with him."

Even while staring at the knife as it sliced through the piece of meat, he could see out of the corner of his eye Glen shaking his head. He managed to ignore it and continue with the meal.

If nothing else, Cooper was real good at ignoring things, his emotions in particular. He had lots of practice at it.

"I figured you'd stop by the arena today, with it being so close and all. Were you busy doing something here?" Cooper changed the subject. Time to put Glen under the microscope for a bit.

"Yeah, I was going to come over, but something came up."

His evasiveness caught Cooper's attention. He glanced up. "Something or someone?"

Glen scowled. "Don't make more out of it than there is."

"I won't, once you tell me what it is."

He let out a breath and looked miserable before he said, "I'm kind of dating someone."

Frowning, Cooper put the utensils down and leaned back from the table to better scrutinize Glen. "How the hell are you dating someone? We had those two girls here all night long just a couple of days ago—" The answer hit him like lightning. "You're dating her? The woman from the other night?"

"Sheila. Yeah, and she's really nice. You'd know that if you ever took the time to talk to girls instead of just finishing with them and then kicking them out."

Cooper raised his brows high. "Excuse me for not wanting the life story of a woman I picked up in a bar and brought home to fuck."

There were women you wanted for a night, and then there were women you wanted to keep around for the long haul. For Glen, that line had apparently blurred.

It didn't mean Cooper had to go along with him though. He decided to make that perfectly clear up front. "I hope you don't expect me to start going out with her friend just because you want to keep seeing this Sheila. If you got any crazy ideas about some cozy double date for the four of us you can get that shit out of your mind right now."

Glen rolled his eyes. "Yeah, because everything's about you, Coop. I can't date a woman without you dating her friend? Please. Sheila's not some buckle bunny from the arena. She doesn't know or care who you are. She actually likes me for me, and not because I happen to be friends with the mighty world champion Cooper Holbrook."

The insult hit home. Cooper drew his brows low. "That's not how things are and you know it."

"Yeah, Coop. It is how things are most times. You just don't see it."

Losing his appetite for dinner and this conversation, Cooper stood. He shoved his plate, uncovered, onto the shelf in the fridge. Beer in hand, he turned toward the doorway. "I'm taking a shower."

After that, he'd have to figure out what to do next. Whatever it was he decided on, it wouldn't be with Glen. Not tonight. Not after that crack his supposed best friend had just made. Didn't matter how well he thought he knew a guy, Cooper realized a man never could tell who his true friends were. He'd have to remember that in the future.

CHAPTER FIVE

Five years later

Glen came out of his bedroom and paused on his way to the kitchen. "Hey. What are you up to?"

Cooper let out a snort. "Nothing."

That could be the answer until the day he died if he didn't get back to where he'd been in his career just a few years ago.

It sucked, the toll time took on a man. Five years ago, he'd been at the top of his game. The best in his sport. Now, he couldn't hang on long enough to qualify to ride in the circuit he used to dominate.

Even Skeeter, the damn kid he'd trained to ride, had gone pro and had a better riding percentage than him this season. It would only be a matter of time before Skeeter would move up from the touring pro division and be ranked in the top forty in the world. Like Cooper used to be. Like he might never be again.

"Fuck." The cuss Cooper bit out as a comment on his whole life in general must have clued Glen in to the full extent of his foul mood.

Glen glanced up and asked, "What's the matter? You've been moping around here and guzzling whisky for days."

"What do you think is the matter?" Cooper scowled. What the fuck? His business partner should know what the hell was wrong. Cooper drew in another swallow and let the whisky burn a path down his throat.

"It's just temporary, Coop. You'll get back on the tour soon enough."

"Yeah, sure. It'll be a breeze. I'll rack up the points and be back just like that." He snapped his fingers. "Top ten. World champion even."

"Maybe it's time you consider retiring."

Maybe it was time Glen minded his own fucking business and went back to the bedroom and that piece of tail waiting on him before Cooper decked him. Still, the suggestion ate at his gut. Enough so he couldn't let it go.

"You saying I should retire because I'm too old to ride anymore?" Cooper asked.

Christ. Maybe it was true since he couldn't keep his points high enough to stay on the tour.

"I'm not telling you anything you don't already know. Bull riding is a young man's game. You're thirty-five. Going on thirty-six this year and that's—"

"Old."

"Yeah, Coop, it is. Considering the level you ride at and the way they're breeding bigger and better bucking bulls every damn day, it is."

Cooper let out a snort and downed more whisky.

Glen watched him polish off the glass before shaking his head. "Retiring from the tour doesn't mean you curl up and die. Jesus, Coop, you'll still be in the business. The ranch is doing great. With you not traveling all over the world following the circuit, we can expand our stock. Hell, you can still ride if you want. Compete locally in the smaller events where the bulls aren't so rank."

Acid rose in the back of his throat at that suggestion. Cooper didn't want to hear logic. He couldn't stomach sitting there and listening to Glen talk about raising bulls. He wanted to fucking ride bulls. Compete in the elite pro circuit he'd ridden in since the year after he'd gone pro when he was just a teenager.

With his former student riding in—and winning pretty regularly—those same local events Glen thought Cooper should be riding in, he could get beat by the kid he'd trained. That would be the final nail in the coffin of his career.

"I'm going out for a while." He stood so fast, the whisky in the glass splashed all over his hand. He transferred the drink to his other hand and shook off the liquid.

"Cooper, you can't drive."

"Sure, I can. Watch me." He turned toward the door, looking at the front table where his truck keys should have been.

"No, you can't. Coop, stop. You're drunk." Glen's voice came from behind him.

Cooper spun back to glare at him. "Fuck you. I'm fine."

"Just stay here with me. We got plenty to drink. You don't have to go out."

The thought that Glen was probably waiting for his girl to come over so they could disappear into his room for the night didn't make his suggestion very enticing.

"Look, I get it. You have a girlfriend. You don't have to go out. Fine. Stay home. Watch TV and hold hands on the sofa if that's what you want to do, but I'm going out."

Glen had been seeing Darla pretty steady for a couple of weeks now. Long enough that Cooper had bothered to learn her name since it looked as if she'd be hanging around for a while. Though if the past was any guide, Glen would date her for six months or so, then they'd break up and he'd move on to the next girl and date her.

The man had turned into a serial monogamist and it was putting a cramp in Cooper's style.

Having a partner who was always in a serious relationship meant he always was going out alone because Glen had no interest in looking for new pussy.

He couldn't count how many nights he'd lain in bed and listened to those two knocking the headboard over the past few weeks. All while he'd been alone. No wonder his temper was extra short nowadays.

Cooper liked the good old days when one-night stands were good enough for both of them. But with his wingman in a relationship once again, it left him to go out alone on the weekends he wasn't riding. It sucked.

"Stop. You're acting like a stubborn ass, Coop. Just sit the fuck down and finish your drink."

Not wanting to give in to Glen, but wanting to finish his drink at the same time, Cooper sat back down on the sofa.

Glen dropped onto the sofa too and let out a sigh.

They sat in silence for a long while, watching the mindless show on television until, during a commercial break, Glen glanced at Cooper. "So, uh, Darla made an interesting comment the other day."

"Yeah?" As drunk as he was, he really couldn't muster much more of a response than that.

"Yeah. She said she wouldn't mind taking us both on at the same time one night. Crazy shit, right?" Glen's gaze cut sideways to Cooper, who couldn't help raising his brows.

"Yup. That is pretty crazy."

"I told her you'd never been into that kind of thing, but she told me to ask you anyway." Glen's pitch rose higher.

In all the years Glen and Cooper had lived together, he'd never heard this tone of voice on his friend and partner. Like a pubescent boy hopeful and scared at the same time.

Cooper didn't know what to make of Glen's reaction to Darla's suggestion, though he couldn't ignore his own. His cock stirred as the idea that next time he heard Darla and Glen getting busy, he could waltz next door and sink himself inside her.

He'd never seriously considered sharing a woman with another man . . . until now.

"I reckon I wouldn't mind." Cooper shot Glen a glance. "Would you? She's your girlfriend."

Glen's eyes widened a bit. "No, I reckon I wouldn't mind."

Cooper's pulse sped, pumping more blood to his already engorged cock. Damn, he was horny. He tried to keep the desperation out of his voice as he asked, "She coming over tonight?"

"I can call and ask her to." Glen's excitement came through his words.

"Yeah, call her." Jesus, they were really gonna do this, and counter to everything he'd ever thought in past, he wanted to.

"Okay." When Glen stood and reached for the cell phone in his back pocket, Cooper couldn't avoid noticing the bulging length outlined in the front of his friend's jeans.

Jesus. Two straight men sitting next to each other on the sofa sporting erections as big and hard as sledgehammers—it was fucked up and the only thing that would make it less so would be a woman between them.

As Glen made the call, Cooper's head spun too much to really listen to the words. All he knew was it sounded as if she was coming over. He got impossibly harder at the thought as he hoped Darla would hurry.

In the meantime, some more liquid courage couldn't hurt. Grabbing the bottle, he poured a healthy splash into his drink and glanced at his friend. Glen nodded and Cooper polished off the bourbon, emptying it into Glen's glass.

Glen disconnected the call and glanced at Cooper. "She's leaving now."

"Good." The single word couldn't adequately express his relief over that.

"So, uh, what made you change your mind?" Glen cut his gaze to Cooper as he reached for his glass. "You'd always been dead set against anything like that before."

Cooper shrugged, not knowing the answer.

"I'm older." Certainly not wiser, but at the moment definitely hornier. "And hell, you and I have been living together for years. It's not like we're not about as close as two guys can get already."

"True. We sure are close." Glen nodded.

This was a messed-up conversation but the thought of

pounding into Darla had him reaching down to adjust the length that was becoming increasingly uncomfortable inside his jeans.

It felt like he'd have the impression of the teeth of his zipper permanently embedded in his dick if he didn't get out of the torturous pants soon.

"Shit." Cooper mumbled the curse but Glen let out a laugh.

"Yeah, I know. Me too." Glen stood and started to unbuckle his pants.

"What the hell are you doing?" Cooper's eyes widened.

Glen glanced at him. "What? Why the fuck should we be uncomfortable? I'm assuming we'll be taking them off soon enough once Darla gets here."

Stripped of his boots and pants, Glen sat again, now in nothing but his T-shirt, boxer shorts and socks. Eyes on the television, Glen sped through the channels with the remote.

He landed on one of the movie channels Glen insisted they subscribe to. It was playing a pretty racy flick tonight. Glen tossed the remote onto the table. He reached for his glass with one hand and his cock with the other.

Cooper couldn't be sure if his friend was aware he was rubbing himself through his underwear or not. Truth was, it was something he really didn't want to think about. But damn, the naked girl on the screen was hot and seeing her roll around with the guy had Cooper itching to reach for his own cock.

He downed the last of the bourbon in two big swallows while watching the actress on TV and thinking about what Darla would hopefully be doing to him shortly.

Staunchly keeping his eyes on the screen, Coop refused to look but still couldn't help seeing the motion in his peripheral vision as Glen continued to stroke himself.

Fuck it. Glen was right. They'd both be naked soon enough, pounding into one end or another of Darla. Cooper denying himself the small relief from the confines of his jeans seemed stupid.

Coop kicked off his boots and then stood to unfasten his buckle and then the fly of his jeans. He was going to stop there but he really was tired of sitting around in his jeans and as soon as Darla arrived, he'd be shucking those anyway.

Drunk enough to be able to ignore how fucked up the situation was, he pushed the denim down his legs and off before sitting again.

Feeling much better, Cooper reached down and adjusted his hardened length through the tight cotton of the boxer.

Cooper heard Glen's intake of breath and glanced over.

Glen's gaze locked onto his, just as Glen reached out, fisted Cooper's T-shirt and crashed his mouth against Cooper's.

The shock had Cooper frozen in place. At least that's what he told himself later when he realized he wasn't doing anything to stop it as Glen shoved his tongue into his mouth.

It was like it all happened in slow motion so that every one of his senses could register the event in vivid detail. The taste of the bourbon on both of their tongues. The way the room seemed to sway, from the drink and the pounding of his pulse. The roughness of Glen's stubble scraping the skin around Cooper's lips raw. Glen's hand landing on Cooper's cock.

That was what broke him out of his shock and had him shoving Glen away with both hands.

The whole thing couldn't have lasted more than a few seconds, but much like in bull riding, those few seconds seemed like an eternity.

Just pushing him away didn't seem enough to undo the horror and anger roiling inside Cooper. Anger at himself for not reacting sooner. At Glen for trying something so fucking crazy in the first place.

Cooper swung at Glen, sending spit and blood flying as his fist connected with the man's jaw. He had to do something to try and undo this feeling of being violated. Betrayed by a man he called friend.

"I understand your girlfriend wanting to fuck me, but

Christ, Glen, I never thought you did." He spoke as he stood and pulled up his jeans. Then struggled to get his boots back on.

"I don't."

"You kissed me!"

"I didn't mean . . . Coop, I swear. I don't know what the hell that was." Glen ran his hands over his face.

Coop let out a snort even as he backed toward the front door. "I think it's pretty obvious what that was."

His friend. His partner. The man he lived with, who he'd pissed in front of without a second thought and who'd seen him walking out of the shower in nothing but a towel, and sometimes in nothing at all, was gay. Or at least bi, since he'd heard with his own two ears the man fucking plenty of women.

"Coop, I'm drunk. It was just a mistake."

Cooper had made many mistakes in his life, but trying to shove his tongue down another man's throat had never been one of them. Teetering on the edge of his fight-or-flight instinct, he realized he was shaking harder than he had in years.

"So what are you? Gay and dating women to hide it? Or hell, are you trying to fuck the gay out of you with your girlfriend?" He could barely get out the last word with his heart pounding so hard it vibrated his throat.

"No." Glen stood there, still in his underwear, looking devastated, but it was too late. The man Cooper thought he knew seemed nothing more than a stranger he didn't know at all.

"I'm going out. When I get back, I want you gone." Realization hit Cooper that it wouldn't be as easy as that.

They were partners in the ranch. He'd have to buy Glen out, and he didn't have that kind of cash lying around. There wasn't enough in the bank and he sure as hell wasn't delusional enough to believe he could win it this weekend in the damn local event he was riding in. He'd have to sell most if not all of the stock and give Glen the money to get out of this partnership.

"Stop. Let's talk about this." Glen took a step forward.

Cooper fought the instinct to take a step back and forced himself to stand his ground.

"Ain't nothing to talk about. Stay the fuck away from me. I want you and all of your shit out of my house by morning." Without even a final glance, Cooper slammed the door shut behind him and stalked toward the truck.

He was too upset and too drunk to drive. He put the key in the ignition anyway, heading for the dirt road on his property. He turned toward the pond, bouncing in the driver's seat as he drove way too fast for the terrain.

Cooper skidded to a sharp stop and parked by the edge of the lake. Cutting the lights, he sat in shock in the dark.

A honkytonk would have been better choice than the solitude. At least there he would have noise and people to distract him.

Instead, he sat alone in the quiet with just the peepers to disturb him. That left him with nothing to do but relive what had happened over and over again until he nearly crawled out of his skin.

He ran a hand over his lips, but he couldn't wipe away the memory.

"Fuck!" He shouted the word while pounding his fist against the steering wheel.

One minute—less even—and his whole life had changed. No business. No friend. All shit added to the stress of his career being in the toilet.

This would be a real good time for a bottle. Maybe in a little bit he'd stop shaking enough to drive and get one. Until then, he closed his eyes and tried not to feel the razor stubble burn around his lips. The memory of it would haunt him forever.

The next thing Cooper knew, his cell phone was ringing. He must have dozed off, though he had no idea how considering the turmoil inside him. Maybe he'd just passed out from the booze.

He fumbled for the phone only to groan when he saw the caller ID read Glen. Against his better judgment, he answered it anyway.

"I don't want to talk—"

"Cooper. It's me." The female voice on Glen's phone, combined with his grogginess, confused him.

"Me who?"

"It's Darla."

"Look, Darla—" Cooper was about to tell her it didn't matter what she had to say, the partnership and the friendship was over, but he didn't get a chance.

Her sharp intake of breath followed by a sob interrupted him. "Cooper, I'm at the hospital. There's been an accident. It's Glen. He's real bad."

CHAPTER SIX

Present day

Hannah walked out of the house and made her way down the path through the tiny but neat flower garden. She opened the picket fence and closed it behind her like she'd done countless times before, but today her hand shook as she secured the latch.

She had to be crazy. Maybe spending half her life as a single, working mother had finally gotten to her. It was the only explanation for why, after ten long years of coveting Cooper Holbrook, she was going over to his house.

What had changed since that night when fate had stepped in and put her on the highway where he'd been stranded? The night he'd kissed her senseless and then told her to steer clear of him. The night he'd walked away from her car and left her wanting and feeling unwanted.

Some very obvious things had changed. Skeeter was ten years older, for one. Now her son wasn't Cooper's student anymore. He was a grown man out on his own, riding in the pro circuit and making a life for himself. But that meant Hannah was ten years older, as well.

Silly that back then, at just thirty, she'd felt too old

compared to the twenty-year-old girls a champion rider like Cooper was constantly surrounded by at the arena. She'd seen one such girl and him in action, live and in person that first time she'd gone to see Skeeter ride.

Now, with her thirties behind her, she knew what it was really like to feel old. Not to mention what it was like being single and living alone for most of her adult life.

At forty, she was starting to have to squint to read really fine print and she'd begun buying better face cream and bras in an attempt to stop the ravages of time on her body.

Yet in spite of all the changes brought about by her turning forty, none for the better in her opinion, it was now that she decided to go see Cooper.

She should have pursued him when she'd been younger. It was a cruel trick in life that youth was wasted on the young. When she had the body, she hadn't had the will. Now she had the will, but it was firmer than the rest of her.

Hannah hiked her boobs higher beneath her shirt, hoping Cooper still thought she had something about her worth his interest.

He'd gotten older as well. Sadly, the steadily revolving fresh crop of rodeo groupies never aged. But he was retired now. No longer on the circuit surrounded by adoring female fans. He didn't go to the arena anymore.

Word was the man didn't go much of anywhere lately, except maybe to town a couple of times a month to stock up on supplies.

That was one point in Hannah's favor—accessibility. He no longer went to the competitions where the girls were, but she could go to him at his house.

Sitting in the driver's seat, she flipped down the visor and glanced into the mirror there. She eyed herself critically, from the laugh lines in the corners of her eyes, to the fact the color of her hair looked duller than it used to.

One good thing from working two or more jobs for the past fourteen years or so since her bastard ex-husband Steven had left her and Skeeter was that there hadn't been much opportunity to abuse her skin sunbathing. That kept any major wrinkles or age spots caused by sun damage away.

Thank God for small favors.

She ran a finger beneath the lower lashes of each eye, wiping away any makeup that might have strayed. She checked her lips and wondered if she should apply more lipstick.

Annoyed at herself for primping for what could amount to an embarrassing mistake on her part, she slapped the visor back up.

Procrastinating wouldn't help her nerves. Neither would more lipstick. Best to just go and face whatever kind of welcome Cooper greeted her with upon her unannounced visit.

The drive didn't take as long as she would have liked it to, and all too soon she was pulling onto Cooper's road.

When she came to the beginnings of the fence of his ranch she saw what her son had alluded to the other night when he'd come home upset after dropping in for a visit with Cooper.

Skeeter had been concerned for his old teacher, and now she could see why. Cooper had really let the place go. A few posts were broken and the fencing was completely missing in one spot.

Not that fencing mattered since it was obvious he had no stock left on the land. The acreage was overgrown with weeds that looked to be waist high and there wasn't an animal in sight.

It was quite a change from the last time she'd been there. That had to have been about five years ago. She'd driven Skeeter to that last lesson before he'd gotten his driver's license at sixteen.

Her son always had been a hard worker. He'd saved up his money from his odd jobs and bought himself a rusty old pickup truck. He'd gotten his license the day the law said he was old enough to qualify, and that was it. No more shuttling him around to rodeos or lessons for her.

Truth be told, Hannah had been disappointed when Skeeter started driving. It meant no more opportunities to run into Cooper. To see him smile and tip his hat when he greeted her, even if that was all the attention she got from him aside from that one embarrassing night.

Maybe it had been for the best that she'd stopped having to see him every time she dropped Skeeter off and then picked him up again. After she'd felt the heat of his kiss that one time, having him treat her like an acquaintance was heart wrenching. Even if he'd given her the excuse that it was better for her to steer clear of him, it hadn't done her ego any good.

No woman, particularly not a single mom, wanted to have an attractive man walk out on her when she'd all but thrown herself at him.

None of it mattered anyway. The lessons with Cooper had stopped shortly after Skeeter had started driving anyway. Cooper had quit teaching, saying he didn't have the time anymore, and Skeeter was juggling school, part-time jobs and riding in every competition he could get to.

Yet here she was, five years after she'd last pulled into this drive, and ten years after that kiss, driving right up to his doorstep. Unannounced, uninvited and most likely unwelcome. She was apparently a glutton for punishment, because she was really going to do this.

Hannah put the car in park and cut the engine, but she couldn't bring herself to get out quite yet. Instead, she sat and stared at the house.

It almost looked abandoned. One front step was broken. A piece was missing from the peeling porch railing.

Was cash so tight for Cooper he couldn't maintain the property? She'd replayed every word of their conversation from that night she'd found him walking on the highway and driven him home. Back then, he'd told her that he spent too much money. Obviously more than was wise, considering the condition of his place.

A good woman in his life might have prevented this from

happening. Kept him on the straight and narrow. Made him not want to drink so heavily or spend so much.

Then again, Hannah hadn't even been able to hold on to her own husband, so what the hell did she know about keeping a man at all? Never mind keeping him in line.

But she did know about good hard work and—after years of living hand to mouth—how to stretch a dollar so far you could see through it. She could help Cooper get out from whatever hole he was in . . . if he let her.

Time to see if he would.

Drawing in a breath to steel her nerves, she got out of the car. She stood tall and marched her pedicured feet right to his front door.

Yeah, she'd painted her toenails and put on her prettiest sandals to come visit Cooper, as if he or any man would notice or care about her toes. She'd obviously lost her mind.

It was too late now. If he were inside, he would have already heard her car. He might have already looked out and seen her there. Leaving now would seem even more foolish than her having come in the first place.

Besides that, her decision had been made. Once she set her mind to something, she didn't let it go easily. Too bad she hadn't done this years ago when she'd been younger and physically better equipped for the job of seducing a man— and before Cooper had fallen so low.

God, how she hoped it wasn't as bad as it seemed, because things looked bad. As if he didn't have the money or the will to keep up the place.

Maybe he had hurt himself and couldn't tend the stock and that's why he'd sold the animals. That scenario was slightly less horrible than him being destitute.

She didn't know what was happening here, but it was time to find out. She raised her fist to the front door and knocked, a little too hard and for much too long.

Peeling paint drifted to the floor in front of her as she pounded loud enough to raise the dead, or at least a sleeping drunk, if that was the case. Skeeter had mentioned Cooper

had seemed like he'd been drinking when he'd seen him.

Hannah didn't want any question as to whether he could hear her knocking or not. If he was in there and not dead or deaf, he'd hear her pounding. If he didn't answer, it would be because he didn't want to see her.

But no, it wouldn't be just her he was trying to avoid. From the looks of things, he didn't want to see anyone. She hadn't missed the no-trespassing sign nailed to the post at the end of the driveway. That was one big clue about his feelings toward uninvited visitors.

As she knocked again, she realized she'd ignored that sign. More than that, she was knowingly outright disobeying it.

"A'ight. Hold your horses! Jesus H Christ, what the hell—" The front door swung wide and she stared into the face from her past.

Cooper's eyes widened as recognition hit.

Hannah's heart pounded so hard it seemed to vibrate her whole body, but she managed to get out two words. "Hi, Cooper."

He glanced past her to the parked car, as if looking to see if she was alone. "Skeeter's not here, if that's who you're after."

She could see him withdraw into himself, almost as if he'd erected a protective barrier between them. He avoided direct eye contact, his focus darting around. He looked anywhere but at her as he ran a hand over his messy head of hair.

Cooper might be embarrassed to have her see him and his place in this condition, but that was too bad. If he still had enough pride to be ashamed, he wasn't past saving, and she wasn't about to give up trying to do just that.

Hannah stepped forward. "I'm well aware Skeeter's not here. I know exactly where my son is. I'm here to see you."

The shock on Cooper's face as he stumbled backward to avoid being barreled over by Hannah would have been comical if this situation wasn't so dire.

He sputtered a second before he finally got out, "What are you doing?"

"I'm coming inside." She swept her gaze over the devastation within the house.

Beer and liquor bottles covered the cocktail table. It looked as if Cooper had been sleeping on the sofa when she arrived, judging by the bed pillow at one end and the indentation of his head still in it.

"Why?" Good thing he was too much of a gentleman to kick her out, in spite of the fact that she could see he didn't want her there.

Hannah turned away from the shambles in the living room and faced Cooper. Even in the dim light she could make out the haze of sleep and booze clouding his bloodshot eyes. "I wanted to see you."

"Why?" His forehead crinkled as he repeated the question.

"I'm old enough that I don't need a reason to do something. Skeeter's grown and gone most of the time. I do what I want nowadays and today I wanted to see you." A strong offense seemed like the way to go in this situation. He looked so shocked he might just be compliant. "So you go jump in the shower and I'll see what's in the kitchen for us to nibble on while we catch up with one another."

Cooper drew his brows lower until they formed one unhappy line. He opened his mouth but no words came out.

Sure it would only be temporary, Hannah decided to take advantage of his speechless state.

"Go." She grabbed him by both shoulders and spun him toward the doorway in the back of the living room.

Hoping that was the general direction of the bathroom, she gave him a tiny shove. He took a step forward and shot her one last confused glance over his shoulder before he disappeared through the doorway.

She had no idea if he'd hide from her and never come back out, or do as she'd said. Either way, she planned to take the time she had alone to clean up this mess.

A man couldn't turn his life right side up in a house that was upside down.

A quick look around the kitchen yielded some crunched-up plastic bags and empty cardboard beer boxes.

She'd just carried all she could find into the living room to start collecting the bottles and trash when she heard the sound of the water running at the back of the house. He was doing what she'd asked.

This crazy plan of hers, which wasn't much of a plan at all, might just work.

CHAPTER SEVEN

Hannah was a nurse full-time and a waitress part-time. That meant she was quick, efficient and not easily rattled or disgusted. She needed all of those traits now as she pawed through what looked like a month's worth of refuse, but she feared was only a few days' worth.

Beer bottles went into the cardboard boxes. Liquor bottles and Coke cans into one bag for recycling. Fast food wrappers, remnants of food and used paper napkins went into another bag of trash.

The T-shirt she found on the floor she tossed into the corner. She'd have to locate the laundry machine and put in a load. She'd bet good money that Cooper hadn't washed clothes in a while. He probably hadn't laundered his sheets or pillowcases in far too long either.

She'd made quite a bit of headway straightening up but still had much to do by the time she heard the water turn off.

Scrambling, Hannah piled the boxes in one arm and scooped up the bags. She carried it all to the front door where she dumped her load onto the porch. She was afraid to take the time to run the bags outside and search for his trash cans. Cooper might see she'd gone out and lock the front door on her.

It wasn't as if she was an invited guest. Once he saw all she'd done, he likely wouldn't take kindly to her meddling or cleaning.

Rushing back inside, she headed for the kitchen to do what she'd said she was going to while he showered—check out the food situation.

She'd managed to ignore the disaster in his kitchen before, when she'd whizzed through looking for the trash bags, but now that was much more difficult to do.

The sink was filled with dishes that looked as if they'd been there for a long while. The garbage pail was full to overflowing and was starting to stink to high heaven.

Blowing out a breath, she headed for the fridge to see what it held. Beer and an old nearly empty bottle of hot sauce. No surprise there. Given all else she'd seen, she hadn't assumed he was stocked with groceries or cooking meals for himself.

Pulling open cabinets, she fared a bit better. There were at least canned goods, though she'd have to wash a pot before she could even start to heat anything. Maybe if she could find a clean bowl, she could microwave something.

She'd just turned around to see if he had a working microwave anywhere when she saw Cooper standing in the doorway.

His hair was damp and his face was clean-shaven. She smiled at the tiny piece of blood-stained toilet paper stuck to his chin where he must have cut himself. He'd even changed into clean clothes, which was a huge improvement over the stained T-shirt and grubby-looking jeans she'd found him in.

Considering the state of the household, she was surprised he had something clean left to wear.

Hoping he couldn't read her thoughts in her expression, Hannah smiled. "You look nice."

Cooper snorted at the compliment. "What the devil are you looking for?"

"A pot so I can heat this on the stove." She held up a can

of beef stew. "Or a bowl if you've got a microwave."

"I'm not hungry."

"Well, I am, and I know you'll want to sit and eat with me. It'd be rude not to." Hannah glanced at the table. "Take a seat. I'll have this ready in a few minutes."

Her full-steam-ahead approach seemed to be working. He still looked unhappy and confused, but he sat in the chair and didn't protest as she rolled up her sleeves and faced the sink.

Figuring she'd better keep him occupied before he decided to kick her out, Hannah scrambled for small talk as she twisted the faucet and hoped at least the water heater still worked in this place. "So you probably don't know this, but Skeeter is staying over at Butch Davis's place."

"Nope. Didn't know."

Not much of a response, but at least it was something. Hannah grabbed a sponge with one hand and squeezed out the last remnants of liquid dish soap from the bottle with her other. "Mmm, hmm. He and some of his friends are there helping out Butch's daughter, Riley."

"Why does she need help? Butch get hurt?"

Uh-oh. This was probably not the most uplifting topic of conversation to be having with a man already down in the dumps. Hannah realized it had been a bad choice of conversational topics on her part.

She turned off the water and spun to face Cooper. "Butch had a heart attack right after the last big event. I'm sorry to tell you this, but he's dead."

A shadow visibly settled over Cooper's features as his gaze seemed to lose focus. Frowning, he stared at something just past her. It was like he was no longer there in mind, only in body.

He was quiet for so long, Hannah was afraid to break the silence and disturb whatever battle raged within him. Then, as if he remembered she was there, he glared at her. "What the hell are you really doing here? That kid of yours send you to check up on me?"

She stood a little taller. "No. That kid of mine didn't even want to tell me anything about you or the condition of your place."

He seemed angry at her comment. "Then why are you here snooping around?"

"Because he was so upset after visiting you I figured I'd better come and see for myself. And don't you take that tone with me, Cooper Holbrook. I'm here to help—"

He stood so fast the kitchen chair tipped over and crashed to the floor behind him. He took a step closer, staring down as he towered over her. "I didn't ask for any help and I sure as hell don't want it."

"Too bad. It's not optional." Chin raised, Hannah returned his glare.

"You need to leave." Nostrils flaring, Cooper might have frightened a less determined woman, but not Hannah.

He could try and look as big and as mean as he was capable of. She could handle it. She'd survived eight years with a husband who liked to intimidate and push her around.

She knew when a man was about to blow and it was time to back down or suffer the consequences. She also knew when a man was bluffing, like Cooper was now. He'd no more hurt her than he would Skeeter, or anyone else for that matter. He wasn't the type.

Hannah crossed her arms and stood her ground. "No. I'm not leaving until you have something decent to eat and I get this kitchen cleaned up."

"What the hell is wrong with you? Why the fuck would you wanna be where you know you're not wanted?"

"If you think cussing at me will help you get your way, you're wrong." Hannah spun back to the sink, leaving him to face her back, though she could still sense his glare boring into her from behind. "Might as well sit and get comfortable, Cooper. We're both gonna be here for a little while."

The sound of the wooden legs hitting the linoleum floor as he righted the chair had her smiling, even if the noise was accompanied by Cooper's annoyed huff.

After a pause so long she considered he might never speak

to her again, Cooper said, "How's Butch's daughter handling it?"

His interest took her off guard, but Hannah did her best to answer as if she wasn't shocked he'd reopened the conversation.

She stayed facing the sink as she worked at scrubbing a pot. "I think she's gonna be okay. Like I said, Skeeter is there at her place in Mississippi now along with a whole slew of the guys. Some of their girlfriends too, so she's not alone. And there's a local hired hand who used to sometimes help her father with the ranch when they were traveling. She can call on him if she needs to."

"She's gonna try and keep the place going?"

"I'm not real sure. I'm not certain if she even knows at this point. It all happened so fast." Then again death, whether it came with a warning or out of the blue, was always hard to handle.

"Stock contracting's a tough job. It's sure no life for a young girl all alone."

"I suppose it's not, but I think Skeeter will be there for her as long as she needs him." It was bittersweet for Hannah seeing Skeeter so grown up and independent. But at the same time, him building a life of his own freed her to do the same.

"It's good he's helping her out. He's a good kid, Skeeter."

Hannah glanced over her shoulder at Cooper and found him picking at a chip on the kitchen table. At least it looked as if he'd accepted she was there for the duration.

"Yeah, he is a good boy. I also think he's got more than a little crush on Riley. Of course, he'd never tell me that. He tries to keep his feelings close to the vest—like someone else I know—but he's not real good at hiding things. I can tell he likes her a lot."

Finally, the old pot was clean enough she wouldn't be disgusted by cooking in it. She put it on the burner and started pulling open drawers.

"Now what are you looking for?"

"Can opener?" She answered as sweetly as she could in

spite of the exasperation she'd heard in his tone.

Kill them with kindness—Hannah had plenty of experience in doing that with the patients and customers at both her jobs.

Cooper stood and she braced for another battle with him, but it didn't come. He moved to the other side of the room, reached behind some beer bottles on the counter and emerged with a hand can opener.

"Ah. Thanks. I wouldn't have thought of looking for it there."

He scowled and sat back down. "It's got a bottle opener on it. I use it to open my beer."

"Oh. Handy."

As he cocked a brow at her comment, Hannah supposed she should be grateful he hadn't chosen to pop open another bottle for himself and drink away his annoyance at her.

She used her nervous energy to open the can, dumped the contents into the pot and turned on the burner.

While that heated, she turned back to the dishes in the sink. "You could take out this garbage while you're waiting. And there's some more trash and recycling out on the front porch that can also go into the bins."

Hannah half expected him to tell her where she could shove her request and the garbage, but he didn't. He grumbled something as he went but grabbed the trash can and pushed through the back door.

When his overwhelming presence was no longer filling the room, she let out a long, slow breath.

Fighting a stubborn man was easier than wondering what a quiet one was thinking. She'd steeled her nerves and had been as unyielding as he was when he'd confronted her. But when he was compliant and looked so down in the dumps like this—that was far harder for her to deal with.

It made her want to wrap her arms around him. Ask him what had happened to bring him to this point and promise to make it all better.

She had to remember that the last thing she wanted to do

was mother this man. Far from it.

If there was anything physical between them, she sure as hell didn't want it to be of the soothing, comforting variety. The contact she'd longed for with Cooper over the past decade had been more of the sweaty, break-the-bed kind.

He seemed to have changed over the years. He wasn't the flirtatious Casanova with the ready smile and legendary skill at charming the ladies she'd known ten years ago, but that wasn't a bad thing.

A little age, a lot of experience, a big change in his life—it must have all worked to calm the wild man he'd been. Hopefully time had made him older, smarter, maybe even ready to settle down.

Settle down. Now she was really getting ahead of herself.

First things first. She washed a spoon and gave the stew a quick stir and then went back to the rest of the dishes. She needed to excavate this mountain and locate a couple of bowls or they'd have nothing to eat out of when the meal was heated.

Cooper slunk back into the room, empty garbage pail in hand. He set it on the floor next to the sink and turned back toward the table.

"Got a bag for that?" Hannah eyed the pail and then glanced over her shoulder at the man who'd starred in her dreams so many nights.

With every fiber of her being, she hated nagging him. Or worse, treating him like a child and ordering him around, but what choice did she have?

She had to straighten this man out so he could get back to living again. At the very least, she had to straighten his place out and hope that started the ball rolling for all the rest. This was the only way she knew how to do it.

He leveled a gaze at her and moved to stand close behind her at the sink. She turned to face him and realized she'd forgotten how tall he was. How small he made her feel when she stood next to him. He'd have to lift her up and set her on top of this cluttered counter for her to be eye level with him.

For her to comfortably reach his mouth and kiss him . . .

That image made it hard for Hannah to breathe.

Cooper planted one hand on the edge of the sink and leaned lower. Hannah parted her lips as her heart rate sped and she anticipated his kiss.

"Excuse me."

Her gaze dropped to his mouth as he spoke before she dragged her focus up to the multifaceted earthy hues that made up the color of his eyes. "Hmm?"

"The trash bags. They're below the sink." Cooper tipped his head in the direction of the cabinet Hannah was blocking.

He hadn't wanted to kiss her. She was just in his way. Once a fool, always a fool.

"Oh, of course. I'm sorry."

A smile bowed his lips, the first one she'd seen in years. It made him look like he had in the past and made her feel just like she had back then. Her breath caught in her throat as he hovered there. Close. Low.

"Hannah, I need to get into the cabinet if you want me to get the bag." He cocked one brow as he said it and she realized she still hadn't moved so he could open the door beneath the sink.

She took a step to the side and then walked all the way around him and to the stove. She needed something to do to cover her embarrassment.

Concentrating on the meal, even if it was canned stew, seemed the best way to distract herself from this attraction that made her look and act like an idiotic schoolgirl. Though she wasn't sure what to do about the overactive hormones that had woken with a vengeance at the mere sight of one of Cooper Holbrook's smiles aimed in her direction.

Hannah shot him a sideways glance. "This should be hot enough for us to eat in a minute."

"A'ight." The slight smile remained on his lips, making him look sexy and devilish, just like the old Cooper.

Her hand stilled on the spoon. "You're not going to fight me about eating?"

"Nope." He whipped the plastic bag open and hung it on the edges of the trash bin.

"Why not?"

Still bent over adjusting the bag, he raised his gaze to hers. "Would it help?"

"Probably not."

"See." He shrugged, slid the trash can to the side and moved back to his chair.

Cooper stretched out his long legs in front of him. Leaning back, he crossed his arms over his chest and focused his eyes on her. The bland expression on his face masked any remaining amusement. That didn't help her discomfort at being under his scrutiny.

With a scowl, Hannah turned back to the stove. The balance of power seemed to have shifted over the past couple of minutes. She didn't like that she no longer felt in control—not of the situation and definitely not of her own damn sex drive.

Stirring the now-steaming stew, she realized she'd never finished the task she'd started when Cooper's closeness had distracted her. Only one bowl was washed. The other remained buried beneath the rubble of dirty dishes. After flipping the burner off, she grabbed the one clean bowl she'd managed to wash. She scooped a good amount of stew into it and planted it in front of him with the spoon.

Maybe with him occupied eating, she'd be able to focus on something besides him.

His gaze swung from the steaming food on the table, to her. "Aren't you eating?"

"I will. Just have to grab another bowl." And wash what looked like a month's worth of dishes.

Ignoring his doubt-filled expression, she turned back to the sink and dug into the pile. She should be able to make some headway on the mess while he ate.

"You know, I'll get to doing those myself."

"Will you?" Hannah imbued the words with a good bit of doubt as she propped a newly washed bowl in the drain board and moved on to the cutlery.

"Yes. Later." Cooper's answer came from directly behind her, making her jump.

When had he stood? He leaned closer and braced one hand on the edge of the counter. She was caught between his body and the sink as he reached past her and turned off the hot water. She felt the heat of his body pressed against her back as he took the wet, clean spoon from her hand.

He moved away to get the bowl she'd washed from the drain board and she felt as if she could breathe again. She turned to watch as he carried the bowl and the spoon to the pot on the stove top. There he scooped her a bit of the stew.

"Come sit." He eyed her where she stood, still frozen at the sink, as he set the food down on the table.

"Okay." She wiped her hands on her jeans for lack of anywhere else dry them.

She sat. So did he.

Eyes focused on the bowl, he dug into the stew and shoveled a large spoonful into his mouth.

Good. That was exactly what she'd wanted—for him to eat a decent meal even if it did come out of a can. And more importantly, for him to stop looking at her and making her feel as nervous as a damned teenage girl.

What she hadn't intended was to fall victim to her attraction to him so quickly. The tremble in her hand as she reached for her own spoon proved she was just as susceptible to this man now as she had been then.

It didn't matter that his championship days were done, or that his ranch had gone to shit both inside and out. The thirty-year-old woman with the unrequited crush on the playboy bull rider was alive and well inside her forty-year-old body.

So much for getting older and wiser. It was clear Hannah had only gotten older. She was still as dumb as the eighteen-year-old who'd gotten pregnant and then had to marry Skeeter's father.

Cooper changed from staring into his bowl to focusing on

her. He cocked a brow and nodded toward the spoon she had yet to lift. "You not eating?"

"I will. It's just a bit hot." The entire kitchen felt warmer since he'd touched her, even if it hadn't been anything more intimate than his getting to the sink around her.

Maybe it was just her face that was warm as the blood rushed to her cheeks. The way her body reacted to this man Hannah might as well have been in puberty.

She remembered the spoon in her hand and took a small bite of stew even though she wasn't one bit hungry.

"So what have you been up to these past ten years?" Cooper making small talk had her bringing her head up in surprise. He cocked a brow and continued, "You said you were here to catch up. So, let's catch up. What are you doing now?"

Being under the close observation of those eyes that seemed to change color with the light along with his mood made it hard for Hannah to think.

Luckily, he'd asked a question she'd be able to answer in her sleep. There was only one possible response. "Working."

"Still two jobs?" he asked.

She nodded. "Yes, but I cut the diner down to one night a week."

His brows knit as he frowned. "That son of yours is making plenty of money riding in the pros. He can help with the bills at home. You shouldn't have to work even one night a week there."

"I don't mind. It keeps me busy. The house feels real empty when Skeeter is away." She let out a short laugh. "And it seems like he's always away somewhere."

"So you're still single, I take it." Cooper's stare remained on her face, making her self-conscious.

She figured he didn't need to glance at her ring-less left hand to confirm she wasn't married or engaged. She'd just told him she was a lonely loser who worked the dinner shift at the diner rather than rattling around her empty house when her son was away, so it must have been pretty obvious she wasn't dating either.

At least she hoped that was the reason he'd assumed she didn't have a significant other, and not because she'd acted like a fainting damsel from just a touch and a smile from him.

"Yeah, still single." Hannah nodded and forced a smile.

"How'd you know?"

"Simple." He shrugged. "Because any man with a brain in his head would want to be with you every night."

Her chest felt tight from the compliment and the blunt sincerity with which it had been delivered. Still, Cooper hasn't said he wanted to be that man in her life. Just that she should have one—one other than him. Same as ten years ago.

Meanwhile, how had the conversation turned to her? She was there for him.

"So what's going on with you?" She knew from the state she'd found him in that it was a loaded question.

Cooper snorted. "You're looking at it."

"No more raising stock? No more giving lessons?"

"Nope." He stared down and dug his spoon into the meat in the bowl.

"Mind if I ask why?"

His gaze whipped up to meet hers. "Mind if I ask you the same?"

The question confused her. "Excuse me?"

"Why are you alone? Why are you taking the night shift rather than going out and meeting someone?"

Because her ex-husband had scarred her so badly inside it felt safer to live alone than risk finding a man who might be worse.

Because she'd been holding on to a flame for Cooper for a decade and he made any other man pale in comparison.

Because after working two jobs—and three for a few years when things were really bad—she was too damned tired to get prettied up and go out to some bar to compete with younger women also trying to meet men. Besides, quality men couldn't be found at a place like that anyway, she was sure.

None of those thoughts came out of her mouth. She

wasn't going to share them with Cooper. Obviously, they both had things they didn't want the other knowing.

Hannah backed down first. "Fine. I won't ask you why you've given up."

He dipped his head. "And I won't ask you the same."

He'd nailed it right on the head with his quick retort. She had given up on having a man in her life . . . until today.

Today, she'd stood firm and the results sat before her. The job wasn't nearly done yet, but he was talking and eating and clean. For less than an hour's work, that was pretty damn good progress, in Hannah's opinion.

It was beyond her to know whether or not getting Cooper back on his feet would mean the two of them could try to have some kind of relationship, but she could hope.

"How's the kid doing?"

To Hannah's great relief, it seemed that Cooper was back to the small talk and was focusing on her son. She could handle that. "He'll be riding in the touring pro event here in Arkansas. You can go see for yourself how he's doing, if you want."

Cooper shrugged. "Maybe."

No matter how Cooper felt about Hannah, she knew he loved her son. She planned to take advantage of that. "Skeeter doesn't come out and admit it, but getting kicked off the tour because of his point ranking was a huge blow to his confidence. He's not sure how to correct what's gone wrong with his riding, but he knows he has to."

"That's why he stopped here the other day? He got dropped from the big tour and wanted me to help him with his riding?"

"I think so." She nodded.

He let out a huff of breath. "I guess if that was what he was looking for, I let him down."

Hannah pursed her lips, not confirming or denying the suspicion.

When Skeeter had first come home from visiting him, he'd been more upset at Cooper's state than his own buck-off streak in his riding. Cooper didn't need to hear that his student was appalled at the devastated condition he'd found his former teacher in, so she kept her mouth shut regarding her real opinion on the matter.

His brows shot high and he released a short, humorless laugh. "Wow. That's the loudest silence I've ever heard."

"Sorry, I didn't mean it to be."

He shook his head. "Don't apologize. I'm the one who bailed on your kid. He came to me for help and, failure that I am, I didn't have any to give him."

"You didn't fail him or let him down. He's concerned about you, yes. But as for his riding, he'll be fine. I think being at Riley's and around the other guys will help get him back on track with his career. Some of the riders with him have been around for a while. They'll straighten him out. He'll be back on top in no time at all, and if he's not? Well then, that means it wasn't meant to be." Hannah shrugged.

Cooper shook his head. "Where's all that faith in you come from? Church?"

Hannah laughed. "No. Life."

A person couldn't live the kind of life she had and come out the other side fairly unscathed without learning to have faith that things would work out eventually. Sometimes you just had to wait a little longer for it than other times, like how she'd waited so long for this visit with Cooper.

Maybe she'd waited too long. Given the state of the place, she had to wonder how he was surviving. With no stock and no job, he had no visible source of income.

She wondered what had thrown him into this bad way to begin with. What had happened to his business and his partner Glen? How long could Cooper live like this?

All of those things, she didn't dare ask. "So, nice weather we've been having."

Cooper raised his sandy brows high. "That's what you're going with? The weather?"

"Got something better?"

"Yeah, I do. How about you tell me what you're really

doing here?"

"I told you. Skeeter was concerned about you." Hannah shrugged.

"That's it? Just your son's concern for his good old teacher?"

"Yes."

"You sure about that?" he asked.

She nodded, lying to him if not herself.

A crooked smile appeared. "I might be off the circuit. Hell, I might have even checked out of life for the past couple of years, but I still know when a woman's interested in me, and you are."

Hannah's cheeks burned from being caught off guard by the truth of his words, even though she knew his tactics well. He always had liked to shock her to drive her away.

"Don't flatter yourself, Cooper."

"Don't lie to yourself, Hannah. What was that over there by the sink? If I'd wanted to, I could have set you up there on the counter and taken you right here in the kitchen and you would have let me."

"No—"

He cocked a brow and she backed down.

Hell, maybe she would have. The man made her molten inside. But the point was, he hadn't done anything more than get the trash bag and serve her some stew, so what she might have done didn't count.

Him not trying anything didn't do much for her already bruised ego except confirm her suspicion that he still wasn't interested in her that way.

She needed to hide this attraction that wouldn't go away. Needed to get things back on an even keel for him and make them not so confusing for her.

Hannah let out a snort. "You're wrong, but since you obviously didn't want to do what you said you could do, it's a moot point now, isn't it?"

"I guess it is." His self-satisfied smirk pissed her off.

Hannah scrambled to prove him wrong. "Look, I'm here

because I owe you a huge debt of gratitude, and so much more for all you've done for Skeeter and for me. He was concerned so I decided to check on you. It's that simple. I pay my debts."

"I'm sure you do." A wry smile lifted the corner of his mouth.

Was that some sort of judgment she'd heard in his tone? "What's that supposed to mean?"

"That I'm sure you always do what's right. I'm betting you've never done a single thing that could even be considered wrong in the slightest."

That certainly wasn't true. That night ten years ago she'd been ready and willing to hike up her waitress uniform and have sex with Cooper in her car, all while leaving her eleven-year-old son home alone while she did it.

"That's totally—"

Cutting her protest short, Cooper stood, grabbed her upper arms and brought her up with him. "Hannah, listen to me. I was no good for you back then, and I'm certainly no good for you the way I am now."

His face was so close to hers as he leaned low that she could smell the remnants of mint toothpaste on his breath.

The man had her locked in a grasp tight enough she'd likely have bruises from his fingers, yet all Hannah could do was take satisfaction in the fact that he must have brushed his teeth when he went to shower.

Had he done it because of her? That had to mean something, in spite of his outward lack of interest.

"You were wrong about that back then." Even as hard as she found it to breathe with him so close holding her like this, she made her point, clear and firm.

"No, I wasn't, but looking back is pointless. So tell me, what about now? Do you admit it's true that I'm no good for you now?"

"No."

"No? Jesus, Hannah. Look around you. What do you see?"

"I see a man who's down but not out. All you need is a little help." Even with her heart pounding so hard she felt it clear through to her throat, she imbued her words with enough passion that he would hopefully believe them.

"I told you, I don't want help." His clenched teeth as he forced the words out enforced the truth of the statement.

"That's half of your problem." Her response was fast and sure and tinged with a little bit of anger as this man continued to frustrate her in all her efforts.

Cooper was silent as he glared at her, until he drew in a deep breath and dropped his hold. Sitting, he picked up the spoon and shoveled some stew into his mouth.

Confused, Hannah stood for a second and then sat herself.

Keeping an eye on him, she tried to figure out what was going on. What had made him give up? Meanwhile, she was having trouble deciding if his compliance was a good thing or a bad thing.

"Eat your stew, Hannah. Then we'll finish up those dishes in the sink together." When she didn't say anything, he glanced up. "Um, hello. Didn't you hear me? What's the matter?"

"I'm not sure what just happened." Why was he giving in? He'd gone from being aggressive and hurtful to completely agreeable in a matter of seconds.

"It's simple." He lifted one shoulder. "I've seen that look before."

"What look?" she asked.

"The determined one Skeeter used to get. Didn't matter how beat up he felt, or how many times he bucked off. He'd brush the dust off, get that fire in his eyes and climb back into the chute. Now I see he gets that from you. I might not know a whole lot, but I know when a fight's not worth fighting. If it will make you happy to wash my dishes, then fine. Wash my damn dishes."

"Laundry too." Hannah crossed her arms as she made her demand.

"No." As his gaze met hers, his tone left no doubt he was against that idea.

"Why not?"

"I'm not letting any woman handle my dirty drawers. That I will fight you on."

"Then you'd better put in a load of laundry yourself while I finish the dishes."

He raised one brow. "What if I tell you the machine's broke?"

"I suppose I'd say I'd like to see that for myself. And if it's true, we can take a trip to the Laundromat in town. That might be better anyway. They have those nice big machines so all your bedding will fit inside one and we'll do your clothes in another."

Cooper sighed like he had the weight of the world on his shoulders, rather than one persistent and moderately annoying woman in his kitchen. "Fine. It's not broken."

"I'm glad to hear it. Nothing worse than a broken washing machine. I've lived through that situation myself once or twice." Hiding her smile, she lifted a spoon of food to her mouth.

As they sat in silence, she ran through her schedule in her head and made a plan to help Cooper continue on the right path she'd set him on. She'd have to run to the grocery store for supplies on her way home, but she'd have time to whip up a quick lasagna with the homemade sauce she had leftover in the fridge. Tomorrow, she could drop that off for Cooper.

No man, no matter how stubborn, could say no to homemade lasagna. That would keep him fed for a little bit. A full belly always did make things seem better. He thought just getting the dishes done would make her happy and get her off his back? Poor Cooper. Little did he know that was only the beginning.

Stubborn, obstinate, contrary—he could try and scare her away all he wanted, but she wouldn't give up that easily. He had no idea what he was up against.

CHAPTER EIGHT

Cooper stared into the bathroom mirror and shook his head at the reflection of his face covered in thick white foam.

He'd gotten into the habit of shaving so seldom over the past few years that the scruff on his chin was more often than not the beginnings of a scraggly beard. Yet here he was shaving. Again. Two days in a row.

Why? Because when she'd left yesterday and promised to *see him soon*, his gut instinct told him he'd be seeing Hannah Anderson again really soon, like today.

He shouldn't—see her again—because even ten years later just seeing her twisted him inside out. Made him want things he wasn't meant to have. Not ten years ago when he'd first met her and certainly not now.

There was a slim chance he could have straightened himself out back then. Maybe. Walked the straight and narrow. Quit drinking. Quit women. Tried to be the kind of man she and the kid needed.

Then, he'd been at the top of his game. His confidence had been as high as the balance in his bank account.

Now? No way. Now was way too late.

Yet knowing that, when she showed up at his door

yesterday, he'd let her in.

In his defense, she'd barreled over him like a bull charging out of the chute. He hadn't really had much choice in the matter. Just like he didn't have a choice about how he felt. How it affected him having her show up after all these years. How she made him want her and hate himself for even considering it.

Hell, hate her too, for looking at him like she did—like he could have her then and there no matter what he said or did. No matter how crappy his life was or his place looked.

Damned woman. Blind to reality and looking to get hurt, she was. As well as nosy, intrusive, domineering . . . and sweet and kind and caring.

He jumped when the blade nicked his chin and watched the red spot blossom as the blood spread into the stark white of the shaving cream.

"Shit." He'd cut himself yesterday and he'd somehow managed to do it again today.

That's what he got for shaving. Served him right. It was just one more reminder that he had no business trying to please this woman because she shouldn't be there in the first place. He certainly shouldn't be worrying whether or not he looked decent when she arrived.

Cooper ran a hand through his overly long hair, thinking he needed to go and get it cut. It had to be a good six months, probably much longer, since he'd bothered going to the barbershop.

He hadn't given a shit about his appearance in a very long time. He shouldn't be worrying about it today. But because Hannah could possibly show up, he'd showered, shaved and put on his only pair of jeans that didn't have holes in them.

It was pretty crazy. She might not even show. Even so, once he'd finished butchering his face, he would go pull a shirt out of the neat stack on his dresser because the damn woman had folded his frigging laundry.

That was after she'd done the dishes and picked up the living room. She'd made up his bed with clean sheets too, even though he'd told her he didn't sleep in it.

He hadn't spent a night in his bedroom for years. Hell, he was barely able to sleep at all, even on the sofa. Mostly he just drank until he passed out. It was the only way he got any rest.

Nope. Hannah hadn't listened to him—no surprise there—so now he had fresh sheets on a bed he'd likely never sleep in. She'd even made him vacuum the carpet while she washed the kitchen floor.

Hopefully, he'd get over this unsatisfied need for her now that she was behaving like a nagging wife. Hell, yesterday she'd acted more like she was trying to be his mother the way she'd fed him and cleaned up after him.

That still hadn't squashed his physical need for Hannah's sweet body. Sad but true, he'd been up half the night thinking about her. That shit was going to have to end. A man like him was no good for her ten years ago and he was no good for her now.

Maybe if he kept repeating that to himself—to her too—one or both of them would remember it. As it stood, he was afraid neither of them did when they were anywhere near each other.

After blotting the blood on his chin with some toilet paper, he went back to shaving in case she showed up.

If she did, it would have to be after her shift at the hospital. Crazy bastard that he was, Cooper still remembered her usual hours from when she used to drop off her son for lessons.

That realization, that he'd been obsessed with this woman for a decade, made him itch to reach for a drink.

Realizing how much he needed one right now—not just as a mental crutch, but physically—he couldn't ignore the tremor in his hand. He wouldn't let himself think the words withdrawal or detox, but the ominous terms hung hauntingly on the edge of his consciousness.

He stuck his head out the bathroom doorway and glanced at the clock that sat on the nightstand next to the neatly made bed he hadn't slept in last night.

It was just past lunchtime. He still had a couple of hours before she came . . . if she came.

Instead of pouring a shot or grabbing a beer to take the edge off like he normally would have, he focused on the razor in his hand.

Swipe by swipe, the blade cut a slow but steady path across his face until he was done. He wiped off any remnants of shaving cream with his newly laundered towel and then turned toward the bedroom.

Grabbing a shirt, he finished getting dressed and made his plan for the day. Not that it was much of a plan. It amounted to him sitting outside on the front porch and waiting for a woman he shouldn't see, who might not come anyway.

After taking one last look at himself, this time in the bedroom mirror, he decided he was as presentable and ready as he was going to get—though ready for what, he didn't know.

Shaking his head at his own foolishness, he made his way down the hall and to the living room. He paused on his way past the doorway to the kitchen. Yesterday, hell, any other day, he would have gone inside and grabbed a cold one from the fridge. Today, he didn't.

Refusing to think about the implications of that any further, he moved out onto the front porch. The same chairs that had been there for years still sat on the worn floorboards. Both the chairs and the floor looked a lot worse for wear, but he supposed he did too after all these years.

He eased his body, stiff and sore from two decades of abuse in the arena, into one of the old chairs. The wood creaked beneath his weight. It would serve him right if the thing collapsed and he ended up sprawled on his ass on the floor.

It was painfully obvious that he'd let things go to shit. His house. The land. Himself. He glanced around him, seeing things in stark reality for probably the first time in years.

He'd gotten real good at turning a blind eye, but today, he took a closer look. Today, he saw things as Hannah would have seen them when she'd visited yesterday. As Skeeter had seen them last week before he'd gone home so upset at the state of Cooper's life he'd gone and involved his mother.

He reached out and flicked at a loose piece of paint on the doorframe with his fingernail. With hardly any effort on his part, a long strip peeled off, leaving raw wood behind it. He picked at another spot with the same results.

In a few minutes, there was a pile of chips on the floor and a good-sized section of the doorframe was bare.

A little work and the whole thing would be clean and ready for a fresh coat.

There used to be some cans of leftover paint in the barn. He'd have to look and see if any of them were still good or if they'd dried up over the years.

Cooper stood and headed for the building he rarely went to since selling the stock. There should be a metal scraper in there too. Maybe even a wire brush or some sandpaper. While he waited for Hannah to show—or not show—he might as well keep himself busy.

Dust and the cobwebs greeted him when he flipped the switch inside the door that controlled the lights in the main part of the barn. Only one light bulb out of three lit. The rest had burnt out, but without any animals around the place, there'd been no need to replace the bulbs. One was all he needed to navigate to the storage closet. After opening the door, he pulled the string hanging from the fixture inside. The single bulb on the ceiling of the small closet illuminated the shelving on the sidewall.

Keeping an ear out for any sounds of a car outside, something he hadn't done for years since company hadn't been welcome for at least that long, Cooper started his search.

He dug through tools in a box on the shelf and found the scraper he needed. There was a flat head screwdriver, as well. That he used to pry open a dusty can of white paint. The contents looked a little thick from age, but it would be fine with a good stir. He replaced the lid and grabbed a hammer to pound it tight.

Pawing deeper into the closet, through things he hadn't had need for in a long while, he found a stir stick and a brush, both from the last time he'd painted, he guessed.

No matter if they weren't new. They'd work for his purposes and save him the time and money of driving to town to buy new. He gathered his finds, pulled the chain to extinguish the closet light and headed for the door.

Squinting through the glare of the sun, Cooper glanced outside at the drive. No car had pulled in while he'd been busy. He had time to get started with his project.

After securing the barn door, he carried his supplies back to the front porch. On his way up the stairs, he realized the railing and the posts needed painting as well. Not to mention the broken step needed fixing.

Hell, the wood was so old the whole staircase should probably be replaced.

One thing at a time. He put down the paint and other things he'd carried. Gripping the scraper in one hand, he set to work.

Less than an hour later, the front doorframe was almost bare and nearly ready for painting. That's when he heard the crunch of car tires on gravel. He turned as Hannah's car pulled into the driveway.

Yup, his guess had been correct. He gripped the scraper a bit tighter, happy to have an excuse to be standing outside other than that he'd been waiting for her.

The work had distracted him, but yeah, beneath it all, the truth was he had been waiting and hoping she'd show.

He forced himself to look casual as she cut the engine and stepped out of the car she'd parked not far from the porch where he stood.

She stared at the doorway and took in the job that had occupied him. "Wow. You've done a lot of work there."

He glanced at the wooden frame. "Nah, it didn't take all that long. Though, these columns and the rail will likely take the better part of a day."

"Well, it looks like a good start." A smile bowed her lips. "I didn't mean to interrupt you, but I wanted to drop something off. It's in my car."

That sounded too much like she was leaving after she'd only just arrived. Cooper didn't know what the thing was that she was dropping off, but as she moved to the passenger side of the car, he scrambled for a way to make her stay without appearing as if that was what he was doing.

"No worries. I'm about ready to take a little break anyway. If you wanted to come in . . . sit and have something cold to drink."

With the passenger door open and Hannah bending over to get whatever she'd brought with her off the floor of the car, all Cooper could see was her ass.

It stuck out temptingly, covered by a denim skirt short enough to lead his eyes to her bare legs and sandals. He swallowed hard. She must have gone home after her shift to change out of her work clothes.

As rude as it was to stare, and at her ass no less, Cooper noticed he didn't feel bad enough about it to avert his eyes.

Christ, he was a pig. Finally, he wrestled his focus away from the temptation, but only because she straightened up and his gaze was drawn to the aluminum foil-covered dish in her hand.

"What the devil have you got?" He hopped down off the steps and moved to reach for the oversized dish she held.

"It's not heavy."

"Well, it looks heavy. And you still haven't told me what it is." He eyed the mysterious casserole dish and grabbed it with both hands.

She finally let him take it. "It's homemade lasagna. I was making one for home and I bought far too many ingredients, so I figured I could just as easily make an extra one. But with Skeeter away, it's way too much food for me alone, so I thought I'd bring it over for you."

"Mmm, hmm." He didn't believe that long cock-and-bull story of hers for a moment.

Hannah had bought too much on purpose, if she had been making lasagna for herself at all and hadn't cooked it just for him.

She was trying to feed him again. What was it with her and food? Of all the physical needs he had, eating was low on the list, especially when he was around her.

Her obsession must come from being a mother. Well, Cooper wasn't her son. Far from it. His thoughts about this woman were in no way how a man would think of a maternal figure in his life. They never had been. Likely, they never would be.

"Come on in." He tipped his head toward the house. "I'll put this monster inside."

Hannah cringed. "I know. It is kind of big, but it freezes real well. You can leave half in the fridge to eat now and freeze the rest for later."

Given the size of this thing, he could feed a football team, so he wasn't sure how she thought he'd be able to eat half all by himself, even if he did plan to freeze the rest. He'd need help . . . and maybe that was her plan.

What if Hannah didn't want him to eat alone? What if her hope was that he'd ask her to join him?

Cooper considered the idea and decided he could deal with that.

Yesterday had been a shock, totally out of the blue. But now that he'd wrapped his head around it, and now that his kitchen was clean and he didn't have to feel like a slob in front of this woman, he could handle spending a little time with her.

It might be nice to hear about how Skeeter was doing with his riding at Butch's ranch.

Yeah, right. Skeeter. That's who he was interested in learning more about.

As she climbed the stairs ahead of him, Cooper attempted to focus his stare straight ahead rather than at how her skirt showed off her curves.

He decided it was best to get his mind off Hannah's body

and onto her food. "I guess I gotta heat this thing up first to eat it, right?"

"I would, if I were you."

"You gonna stick around and make sure I don't mess it up? Maybe stay and help me eat some of it?" He eyed her as she opened the front door for him to walk through carrying the pan.

"Um, sure. I can do that. I don't have any work tonight. If you're sure."

"Of course, I'm sure. I've got all those clean dishes. Might as well use 'em." He led the way to the kitchen, glancing back at her as he set the dish on the counter.

Her cheeks colored at his comment. "Sorry that I kind of took over uninvited yesterday."

As if today she had been invited?

If only he could figure out what her end goal was. The mixed vibes she gave off weren't clear.

He didn't know whether she wanted to take him to church to save him or take him to bed and screw him—maybe both. The strangest part was he was starting to suspect he might not fight her on either one.

"It's fine." Cooper shrugged, dragging his wandering mind back to her concern about busting in on him to clean and cook.

Since he'd been waiting on her to arrive, he figured he must not mind the uninvited company as much as he thought he would, or as much as he would if it had been anyone else who'd shown up at his doorstep two days in a row.

He reached for the handle of the fridge and glanced back at Hannah. "Want some sweet tea?"

She raised her brows. "You have sweet tea?"

"Yeah. I made it fresh last night."

"Um, sure. All right."

At her expression of doubt, he laughed. "I moved away from home and started living on my own when I was sixteen. It was either starve or learn how to do lots of things."

The least of which had been how to make the perfect,

homemade sweet tea. He put the sugar in while it was piping hot so it would dissolve. Some folks he knew were adamant about not chilling it in the fridge, but Coop liked his tea cold so he could drink it without adding any ice. That way the flavor didn't get watered down.

Of course, he hadn't bothered to make tea in years. Beer had been his choice of beverage to quench his thirst and whisky his choice to blur his mind and dull the pain, both physical and emotional.

"I didn't know that about you."

"That I could make tea?" he asked.

Hannah smiled. "That too, but no. I hadn't realized that you'd moved out and were on your own so young."

He shrugged. "I was riding the pro circuit full-time at seventeen, so it wasn't like I was alone for long. Back then, on the road we'd cram as many guys into a single hotel room as we could without getting kicked out."

Strange as it seemed, those felt like the good old days. He'd been poor as dirt and living hand to mouth. Back then, he juggled paying for fuel and lodging and food with whatever was left over after covering the entry fees to ride.

Christ, he missed those days, back when he had more friends than he could count and a good dose of blind faith.

He knew things could only get better and they had. He'd reached the top but realized that once he did, there was nowhere to go except down.

Cooper glanced up and realized Hannah was watching him. "So, what do you need me to do with this thing?" He tipped his head toward the lasagna.

"Does your oven work?"

He let out a short laugh. "I guess we'll find out, won't we?"

"You don't know?" She raised her brows above those eyes he wouldn't mind staring into for a few hours . . . or days.

Cooper yanked his mind off that image and shook his head. "Nope. Generally, I'm not here baking pies or cookies or whatever people make in their ovens. If it can't be fried in my cast-iron skillet, I usually don't bother eating it."

She shook her head. "And yet you're still in perfect shape."

He was surprised, as much at the unexpected compliment as how her gaze swept over him. "Perfect, huh? Do you need glasses, woman?"

"Not quite yet, but probably soon enough." Hannah shot him a cocky look over her shoulder as she flipped the dial on his oven. "It's cooked, but it's going to take a little while to heat through."

"Okay." Of course there was the microwave, which could heat up two slices quick, but Cooper didn't feel the need to mention that.

She was the chef here, but more importantly, only a stupid man would cut the evening short on purpose. Though he had been known to be stupid in the past, he was finally learning.

"Oh, I forgot." She spun towards him. "I've got a salad in the car."

"A salad?"

"Yeah. Nothing special. Just tossed lettuce with tomato. And cucumbers. And some dressing." Hannah shrugged, but Cooper saw through her ruse to make light of it.

She'd planned an entire dinner for him and her. Or at least for him, but she didn't look as if she was going anywhere now, so maybe this was some sort of a date.

"You buy too much of all that stuff too?"

"Yup." She nodded.

His lips twitched at her answer. Her guilt over lying sounded loud and clear to him. "A'ight. I'll run out and get it from your car."

"Okay. It's in a bag on the backseat. Grab the bread too."

"Bread too. Got it." He smiled broader.

Yup. It seemed she had the whole meal covered and he wasn't going to argue with her over it. He'd accept her food.

It was the rest he couldn't accept, because he had a feeling what would come next. If he was right, first Hannah would lure him in with the meal. Before he knew it, he'd be tempted to share much more with her than just food.

He only hoped he was a strong enough man to resist an enticement that great. Maybe after he was fueled up on her home-cooked dinner, he'd have the strength.

Of course, Hannah's lasagna could prove that the best way to a man's heart was through his stomach. Good thing he was pretty sure he didn't have a heart. He just had to keep his dick in check and he'd be good.

He opened the door of her car and found the bag. Opening it, he saw there was indeed a salad in a plastic bag, all made and ready to go. And there was the bottle of dressing, as well as the bread she'd spoken of, all wrapped in foil and smelling of garlic, that he supposed she planned to bake.

Accidentally bought too much, his sweet ass. Hannah was monumentally bad at lying, and he liked her even more for it.

Christ almighty, he could love this woman, if he believed he was capable of that emotion. If he had something more to offer her than an overgrown ranch and a man past his prime, he might even give it a try.

CHAPTER NINE

Hannah swung the car into Cooper's drive for the third day in a row. The closer she got to the house, the more her heart sped.

This was crazy. Stalker kind of crazy. He was bound to know she was lying, showing up at his house twice with the same excuse—that she had too much food for just her to eat alone.

She needed to come up with something better. As her brain spun, the brightness of the fresh white paint on the railings of the porch caught her attention.

He'd done more work on the place. He was taking pride in his home.

That had to be a good sign. As was the fact she'd found him sober, clean-shaven and dressed in decent clothes yesterday even though she'd arrived unannounced. He was taking pride in himself as well.

Maybe she was a fool for still chasing after this man after all these years. It might amount to nothing but embarrassment for her, but she couldn't help but think that her sudden reappearance in his life had knocked him out of the hole he'd fallen into. If nothing else came of all this, that at least would make it worthwhile.

The front door swung wide and Cooper swaggered onto the porch. It was too late to turn tail and run now. Besides, what would she do with the gallon of chili sitting in the cast-iron pot on the floor of the passenger side? As it was, it was more than the two of them could eat tonight.

If he hadn't already, he would soon figure out her plan. She intended to fill his freezer and make sure he was well fed. Well, that and spend more time with him.

Hannah cut the engine and braced herself. One of these days he could very well tell her to get lost. Send her home, food or no food.

Hell, he'd sent her away the night they'd kissed and his hand had been up her skirt at the time. Why she thought now would be any different, just because she came bearing chili, was beyond her.

Swinging the door open, she pasted on a smile. Her heart racing, Hannah stepped onto the gravel and glanced at the man on the porch. "Hey."

He moved to the top of the stairs and dipped his head in greeting. "Hey, yourself."

"So, I uh made chili and I brought you some."

"Did you now?" The corners of his lips crooked up higher in a smile.

"Yup." She walked toward the passenger side and opened the door.

Cooper hopped down the steps and came toward the car. "Let me help you with it. Knowing how you like to cook enough for an army, I'm sure it's heavy."

She glanced up, caught his grin and had to smile herself. She wasn't fooling anyone, but maybe it didn't matter. Judging by Cooper's broad smile and the way he'd dug into last night's lasagna, he didn't mind.

She hadn't minded last night's shared meal either. She hadn't been there for very long. Considering she'd been uninvited, she hadn't wanted to overstay her welcome. She had left right after they finished eating and had done the dishes.

But their short time together had felt far more relaxed than the first time she'd shown up. As if he'd expected her to come and hadn't minded her intrusion all that much.

They'd talked, mostly about the one thing they had in common—her son. She told Cooper what Skeeter had told her during their daily phone call. About how things were going at Riley's place.

Hannah had probably been at Cooper's less than two hours total, but it had been nice. Too nice. She shouldn't get used to it because who knew when it would end?

Not arguing with him about carrying in the chili, she stepped aside so Cooper could get to the pot. "It's right there on the floor."

He bent to grab the cast-iron pot filled to the top, lifted and let out a groan. He glanced up at her. "You shop for a whole side of beef for this thing?"

She shrugged. "The big-size package of ground beef was on sale so . . ."

Grinning, he shook his head. "A'ight. Let's get this inside and on the stove."

"Let me grab the corn bread."

He cocked one brow. "Corn bread too?"

"Can't eat chili without corn bread, now can you?"

"No, I guess not. No more than you can eat lasagna without garlic bread." He smirked.

"Exactly."

Cooper shook his head and turned toward the porch. "Watch the rails. Paint's still drying."

"Okay. Will do." Grabbing the basket of corn bread off the seat, Hannah tried to quell her fluttering heart.

All the changes in the past few days weren't lost on her. Cooper was slowly but surely fixing up the house. He'd smile now when he saw her rather than frown. He didn't argue with her attempts to make sure he was well fed.

She hated to say it and jinx herself, but things were going well. So far, so good.

Keeping away from the railing, Hannah followed him up the stairs and into the house.

Cooper set the pot on the stovetop and turned on the burner. "Something to drink?"

"Sure. Thanks."

"Beer? Or sweet tea?" He paused with one hand on the handle of the fridge waiting for her answer. She hesitated long enough, Cooper finally let his hand drop and turned fully to face her. "Hannah, I'm not an alcoholic. Yeah, I drink more than I should, but I can have one beer, or even two, and stop there. You don't have to worry. You and I can have a beer with our chili. It's not going to send me on a bender. I promise you."

That was exactly what she'd been afraid of. Finding him completely sober these two days had made her happy that he was getting his life together, but it had also made her wonder if it was all-or-nothing with him. If he had to be stone-cold sober, or drink until he passed out.

"That's fine. I'll just have tea."

"A'ight." He opened the fridge and took out the tea and a beer.

She tried not to react but knew most times every thought she had showed on her face. She accepted the glass of tea he poured for her. "Thanks."

"You don't believe me." His lip lifted in a sneer as he pried the cap off his bottle.

She decided the best course of action was to play dumb. "Don't believe you about what?"

"You know about what. But it doesn't matter, because I'll prove you wrong." He set the bottle down with a clunk and braced his palms on the table to lean toward her. "You working at the hospital tomorrow?"

Her mouth had gone dry from nerves over how near he was as he bent close to her. Hannah swallowed hard before she answered, "Yes."

He nodded and then straightened up, grabbing his beer as he did. "Fine. You show up here bright and early on your way to work and I'll cook you breakfast."

"Cooper, you don't have to do that. It would be insanely early. Before seven."

"Yeah, I do have to do this. I want you to see I'm telling the truth, and short of you spending the night here to witness it, you coming over tomorrow morning and finding me bright-eyed and bushy-tailed is the only thing I can think of that will prove it to you. I can have a couple of beers and stop. I promise you."

"Okay."

He scowled and shook his head. "You'll see, Hannah."

Her very short answer must have made Cooper think she didn't believe him. Little did he know it was the idea of her staying the night there with him that had her heart pounding so hard she couldn't manage to say more.

Did she believe him about his drinking? With every fiber of her being she wanted to.

"Okay," she repeated and moved toward the stove. "I'm gonna stir this so it heats through."

"Fine. You do what you need to do, and I'll do what I have to."

She could see he hated that she doubted him. His scowl remained firmly in place as he took a slug of beer.

What he didn't realize was that she had lived with a drunk for a long time. She'd heard all the promises before. Heard the lies too.

It wasn't fair to judge Cooper based on Steven's behavior, but that had been Hannah's life for so many years, it was hardwired into her to expect the worst.

She'd found Cooper and his place battered and bruised around the edges, but she was just as broken. The only difference was her damage was much older and only on the inside where no one could see it.

"So you gonna be here in the morning?" Cooper made it sound more like a dare than a question.

"Yes."

He nodded. "A'ight then."

The jovial atmosphere was good and broken. Now the pall of doubt hung in the air between them.

The responsibility for that lay square on her shoulders because she couldn't hide her feelings well enough. Maybe that was all right though. She'd hid too many emotions over the years. It was good she couldn't hide anything from Cooper.

This atmosphere didn't bode well for a pleasant meal however. She'd have to fix that. "So Skeeter called me today and was telling me about the training he's doing over at Riley's. Apparently, all the guys are now taking daily yoga classes."

His gaze shot up. "Yoga? Who exactly is doing this?"

"Chase Reese is running it, but the other riders there are Aaron Jordon, Garret James, Mustang Jackson and Slade Bower. And of course, Skeeter too."

"Mustang and Slade are doing yoga?" Cooper raised his brows.

Hannah smiled at his reaction. "Yup. Apparently, Chase is kicking them all into shape."

He shook his head. "Tell that kid of yours I'd like to see a picture of this yoga class."

"How about I try and get you a video?"

Cooper chuckled. "You do and I'd love you forever."

Her pulse raced at hearing those words from Cooper's lips, even in the context of a joke. She tamped down her juvenile response and nodded. "Then I'll have to see what I can do about getting one."

"When's that touring pro event he's riding in?"

"This weekend."

"In Springdale?"

"Yeah, I think that's what he said."

"You going?"

"I can't. It's my weekend at the hospital. I'm trying to switch with someone, but we've got a nurse out on maternity leave so staffing is extra tight."

Cooper nodded. "I might just check it out myself."

God, how she wished she could go with him. Then again, retired or not, Cooper was still a former champion and a good-looking man. The groupies would probably be all over him, and she wasn't sure she could handle seeing that again.

"I think Skeeter would love to see you there."

"Well, I don't know about that, but maybe if I watch the kid in competition, I can figure out what's gone wrong with his riding." He took another sip from his bottle.

"That's a very good idea." Things were well on the way to being back to normal. Or at least the way they were last night, before she'd doubted him. As the fear that she'd find him passed out or hung over when she arrived in the morning settled in her gut, she turned to him where he sat at the table. "This is just about hot enough to eat. Can you grab me two bowls and spoons?"

"Sure thing."

As he stood, she eyed the level of liquid inside his bottle, but the glass was dark and she couldn't see. It didn't matter anyway. After she left tonight, he'd either drink until the fridge was empty of every beer inside or he wouldn't. Only time would tell.

When she glanced up, she saw by the expression on his face and how he shook his head that he'd caught her looking at the bottle. "You better be here tomorrow morning, because I'm gonna be up and waiting on you, and I won't take kindly to being stood up."

Swallowing hard, Hannah nodded. "I'll be here. I promise."

CHAPTER TEN

The morning light streamed through the window and made the tiny dust particles visible as they danced in the air. Cooper noticed them as he led the way from the front door and into the kitchen.

He supposed the dust couldn't be helped. He'd kept the house straight and fairly clean the past few days, but he'd never be able to make it spotless or dust-free. This was a ranch house in Arkansas during the dry season. Dirt and dust happened. He pushed concern over the state of the house out of his mind and leaned against the edge of the counter.

Arms crossed, he waited and watched for Hannah's reaction.

She paused in the doorway to the kitchen. Her gaze went to the table and the wildflowers he'd stuck—for lack of a vase—in an old glass pitcher he'd found in the cabinet.

It wasn't the flowers he wanted her attention on at the moment. It was the refrigerator and his sober state. He pushed off the counter and turned toward the fridge.

He glanced at her over his shoulder as he yanked open the door. "Come here."

"Cooper, you don't have to—"

"Hannah, please come here." He waited for her to comply before saying, "Four bottles still in the fridge in the six-pack holder. Two empty bottles in the recycling bin. No hangover."

She stayed where she was as he slammed the fridge door shut. "Cooper, I never said—"

"I know you never said anything, but you thought it. Thought it so damn hard I could see you thinking it."

"I did and I'm sorry." The sincerity was clear in her voice. Her honesty had him softening a bit as it chased away some of the anger her mistrust in him had caused.

"It's a'ight. The way you found me here that first day, can't say I blame you."

Hannah lifted one shoulder. "I did show up uninvited."

"You sure as hell did." And he was glad she had.

Her gaze met and held his for long enough he felt himself falling deeper into this woman. It sure as hell didn't help that he'd been kept awake with mental images of her for hours last night.

The way he was feeling now with her looking so vulnerable and contrite, it would be too damn easy to make her late for work.

Finally, she broke her gaze away from his. "Nice flowers."

"Found 'em growing in the field that I'm fixin' to brush-hog. Figured they were too pretty to mow down so I picked 'em."

He still had to replace some boards on the porch, but he'd decided to postpone that and tackle the overgrown fields first. If he wanted to put stock in those fields again, he needed to knock down the tall weeds so some grass could grow.

Of course, he'd also have to check all the fencing and make any repairs necessary. There was a lot of work ahead of him.

"Cooper Holbrook . . . picking wildflowers." She smiled prettily.

He laughed. "Stranger things have been known to happen.

Such as Cooper Holbrook baking muffins."

"You baked muffins?"

"I did." He tipped his head toward the oven pumping heat into the kitchen.

She grinned wider. "Good thing we found out your oven works."

"Good thing." He nodded in agreement. "So that local touring pro event Skeeter's riding in, which day is it this weekend?"

"Saturday."

"You still not going?" he asked.

"Probably not. I'm trying to change my schedule, but it's doubtful. The weekend shifts at the hospital are always hard to get coverage for. The nurses with children like to have the day off to go see their kids' games."

"You have a kid competing too."

"I do, but he's not exactly a child anymore."

"I guess." He felt more disappointed in her answer than he could have imagined.

He'd built up in his mind a whole scenario where they went to the event together. It would be as close to a date as he'd come to in pretty much ever. Although, all these meals they'd been sharing were sure taking on a date-like feel. Especially now he'd put those damn daisies on the table.

"Are you still planning to go?" she asked.

"Yup. It's been a long while since I've seen the kid ride. It should be interesting."

"No doubt." She smiled. "And I'm sure he'll love seeing you there."

He hoped so. Cooper hadn't left the best impression last time Skeeter had been there. He needed the kid to see him looking better than the last time he'd shown up uninvited—much like his mother had a few days ago when she'd woken him out of a dead sleep as he was coming off a drunk.

The one consolation was that he hadn't gotten that liquored up since the day Hannah had busted into his house. He didn't know if he was straightening out his life to please

Hannah, or Skeeter, or himself.

Things were a jumble in his mind. Everything seemed so confusing.

His attraction to Hannah hadn't faded with the years. He wanted her now as much as he ever had back then. He was pretty sure she felt the same. But instead of keeping her at arm's length like he'd done in the past because he knew he wasn't any good for her, he'd invited her over for breakfast.

Jesus, he must be losing whatever sanity he had left. He'd baked muffins and picked friggin' flowers for the table. All for Hannah.

The logical thing to do—the best thing for her—would be to cut her loose completely. He needed to back away from this woman and never see her again. The problem was that was the last thing he wanted to do.

All this thinking was more than he could deal with this early when he'd been up at five getting ready for Hannah's arrival. "Coffee's made. I wasn't sure how you took it, so I ran out to the store last night for milk. That's in the fridge and sugar is on the counter. There's tea bags too, if you prefer hot tea over coffee."

"Thank you. Coffee's fine."

"A'ight. Help yourself." He wrapped a dish towel around his hand and concentrated on pulling the muffins out of the oven without burning himself.

He didn't own a potholder. No surprise there. He hadn't used the oven until Hannah showed up with her lasagna. He'd never bought muffin mix either.

A handful of visits from this woman and his entire life seemed different. That alone should have sent him running. It hadn't. Go figure.

"Can I pour you a cup?" she asked.

"Sure. Black. Lots of sugar."

"Okay." She poured a second cup. She even got a spoon out of the drawer and put the sugar in it for him before she carried both mugs to the table.

For a man who'd spent quite a bit of time with many

women doing all sorts of things, it was baffling how simply sitting down to a cup of coffee with this one could affect him so.

Maybe it shouldn't surprise him. He hadn't done this before—the whole breakfast and coffee thing.

He'd sidled up to a bar with many a female. He'd tumbled into bed, or the truck, or onto the sofa with them too. Then he'd get them out as fast as possible. If they stuck around until sunrise, he'd make sure they didn't settle in for the day by getting them out right quick in the morning.

This might possibly be the first breakfast he'd willingly sat down to with a woman. He liked it and he hadn't even gotten the night of sex before it.

He tore off two paper towels for them to use as napkins since with all the stuff he had bought last night, he'd still forgotten to get those. He didn't feel too bad. Hannah should be used to this by now. They had been wiping their mouths with paper towels for the last three days she'd been there.

That thought made him realize that this was day four of having her in his life. He also realized he was starting to get used to seeing her.

Yeah, it was decision time. Move forward or step back. This limbo in the middle with them both pretending there was nothing between them couldn't last forever. Both of them could get attached, and when he stepped away, like he always did, she'd get hurt.

So would he. He'd miss this if—when—it stopped.

That right there was reason enough to never see this woman again. To tell her here and now thanks for all she'd done for him, but she shouldn't come by again. If he said it, there was a chance she might actually listen and do as he asked.

That's what he should do. Instead, he said, "Need me to bring Skeeter something when I see him at the event?"

"I don't think so, but I'll ask when I talk to him and get back to you, if that's okay?"

"Sure. If he does, you can drop it by here or I could come

pick it up at your place after you get off work."

"Okay, thank you. I'll let you know."

"A'ight." Now he was offering to go to her house. Yup. He'd clearly lost his mind. Cooper grabbed a hot muffin out of the tin and tossed it onto the paper towel in front of him. "Dig in before they get cold."

Sometimes things were too far gone to save. His resolve to stay away from this woman was very possibly one of those things.

~ * ~

Hannah looked up from the chart on the desk and caught her coworker on this shift watching her.

"Did you need something?" she asked.

"Yeah. I suppose I do." Jillian nodded. "I need to know his name."

"What? Whose name?" Hannah laughed, even as the flush of guilt warmed her cheeks. Was she that transparent?

"Come on. Spill it. You haven't looked so happy in . . . ever. You've started wearing makeup to work. You never used to do that. And did you get highlights in your hair?" Jillian frowned as she zeroed her attention in on the top of Hannah's head.

Hannah reached up to touch the hair confined in the tight bun. "No. I mean, yeah, but I did them myself. One of those home box jobs. It's no big deal."

Jillian let out a snort. "The hair and makeup may not be a big deal, as you say, but the reason behind all the changes must be. So tell me, who is he and what's going on with you two?"

"There's nothing going on."

Sadly, that was the complete truth. Nothing more than two people sharing some dinners . . . and one breakfast. No more than that, in spite of the makeup she found herself applying each morning and the new highlights she had gone crazy and put in her hair.

"I'm going to make a bet that under those scrubs you're wearing your nicest bra and underwear. Am I right?"

Jillian obviously wasn't letting this topic drop. Hannah felt her cheeks burn hotter. She did have on her best underthings. Apparently, she couldn't hide a damn thing from anyone.

Hannah glanced up and saw Jillian still waiting for an answer. She finally gave in. "All right. He's a guy I knew years ago."

"He's an old flame?" Jillian's eyes grew wide. "How exciting."

She wished that were true. "No. Not an old flame. Just a guy who used to give my son lessons. I uh, ran into him recently." Ran into him when she went knocking on his front door. "Anyway, nothing is going on."

"Nothing is going on yet." A smile spread across Jillian's face. "You keep upping your game like this and that won't last long."

Hannah dismissed the idea with a wave of one hand. "I don't know. I'm not sure he's interested."

"Why the hell wouldn't he be interested in you? You're smart, funny, attractive, hardworking, kind—"

"That's the nicest thing anyone's said to me in . . . forever. Maybe I should date you." Hannah laughed.

"Sorry. Possession of a penis is a must in whom I date. That's a deal breaker for me." Smiling, Jillian shook her head. "But seriously, just give this guy time. Some men require lots of patience. Luckily, we've got lots of it."

"We who? Women?"

"Nurses." Jillian grinned.

"That's the truth." Hannah snorted out a laugh. Patience was one of the requirements of being a nurse. She touched her hands to her cheeks, still embarrassed that people had noticed the changes when she'd thought she'd been so subtle. "You don't think the makeup's too much, do you?"

"No. Not at all. You look great. You start looking any better and I may have to rethink my penis requirement." Jillian grinned and winked.

Hannah laughed. "Thanks."

One of the doctors pushed through the swinging doors of

the unit. "We need everyone available in the ER. EMS just called it in. School bus overturned. Multiple casualties on their way. They'll be here any second."

A school bus. That meant those injured, possibly dead, were children. Her chest tightened at the thought. Accidents were always bad, but children made it seem all the worse.

The doctor turned and she ran to follow, Jillian at her side.

The sight as she entered the emergency room stole Hannah's breath. "Oh, my God."

Gurney after gurney pushed through the door, every one with a tiny figure on it, each child looking more terrified than the last.

Harder to see than the ones who were screaming, were the ones who remained silent. She hoped they were motionless because they were unconscious and not the alternative.

She snapped herself out of the shock the horror caused. Now wasn't the time to think like a mother. Now was the time to rely on her training and years of experience as a nurse.

Hannah moved to the nearest curtained enclosure and the wailing child inside. She pulled back the sheet to see the source of the blood soaking through. A broken bone protruded through the skin of the girl's arm.

They were going to need to operate, but the question was how many more needed the same? They had to take the time to evaluate the extent of all the injuries, prioritize and take care of those in life-threatening situations first, while making the rest as comfortable as possible in the meantime.

"It's okay, baby girl. It's going to feel better soon."

As the child screamed for her mother, it brought Hannah right back to the time Skeeter had been that little.

He'd climbed a tree that was way too big for a boy his age, fallen and broken his arm. She remembered the nausea she felt at first hearing the sound of his screams. The pounding of her pulse as she ran to him and saw him lying on the ground, his face deathly pale, his limb twisted. No amount of training had prepared her for what it felt like to see her own child hurt.

Hannah moved past the wrenching of her heart as all the visceral memories came back full force. There was no time to get emotional now. There was too much to do. But she was sure that later, when she was all alone, the images and the sounds of these children would haunt her and rob her of sleep in that empty house she called home.

CHAPTER ELEVEN

The phone rang a little while past the time Hannah should have gotten off her shift at the hospital. Maybe she'd run home after to change, or possibly to whip up something for dinner, and now wanted to know if she could drop by.

Liking that idea, Cooper smiled as he answered the phone. "Hello?"

"Hey." Hannah's soft greeting coming through the earpiece did things to him.

Her voice funneled directly into his ear and seemed to cut through him, straight to the core of his need. He'd wanted her for so long, that shouldn't be a surprise. What was a surprise was the clenching of his heart when he heard her.

"Hey, yourself. Done with work? You on your way home?"

"I was, but . . ." She hesitated before continuing, "Would you mind if I stopped by your place?"

"Of course not. Not at all." He'd like nothing better than to have her there with him.

"Are you sure? I don't have any dinner with me."

Cooper let out a surprised laugh. "Hannah. I don't let you in the door because you bring me dinner."

"But it's dinnertime and I just invited myself over."

"And I'm pretty sure there are a few pieces of that lasagna from the other night still laying around here somewhere for us to eat." He knew there was some in the freezer and still more in the fridge.

The way she liked to cook in volume, there was probably enough for two more dinners and a few lunches leftover.

"All right. I'll be over in a few minutes."

"I'll be here. See ya then."

"Okay. Bye."

He disconnected the call and sat for a moment, phone still in hand. She hadn't sounded right. At least, not as she normally did. Something was going on.

Getting up and heading for the fridge, he figured guessing would do no good. He'd find out soon enough when she got there. Until then, the least he could do was start the meal heating and set the table.

He'd only just gotten the leftovers into the microwave when he heard her car in the driveway. She must have called from right down the road. He set the timer for it to cook for a few minutes and then headed for the front door.

Out on the porch, he watched her get out of the car. Her expression told him as much as her tone on the phone had. She looked drained. Beaten down.

Something was up. He made himself wait for her to come to him.

When she reached the stairs, she glanced up and forced a smile. "Hi."

"Hi. Come on up. Dinner's in the microwave."

"Okay, thanks." She looked less than enthusiastic about eating.

From the look of her, like she was ready to drop, he could imagine food was the last thing on her mind. She reached the top step and stepped onto the porch.

The moment they were on the same level, Cooper reached out and laid his hands on her shoulders. "Tough day?"

"Yeah." She stepped closer, her eyes on his. He saw the

anguish in them.

"Jesus, Hannah. What happened?"

She drew in a breath. "Bad accident came into the ER."

"Wanna talk about it?"

She shrugged beneath his hands. Not exactly an overwhelming response.

"Need a hug?" he asked.

"God, yes."

Cooper pulled her closer. She dropped her head and rested her forehead against his chest.

They'd spent a lot of time together lately. She'd found him at a pretty low point in his life, and she'd stuck it out to see him working his way back to becoming a decent human being again. But they'd never had close physical contact.

Not since that night in her car ten years ago. And never like this—this purely platonic comforting kind of contact. But the least he could do was give her his shoulder to lean on. Or his chest, as the case may be.

He leaned his cheek against the top of her head and rubbed his hand up and down her back. It felt both natural and strange having her in his arms. He was used to holding women as a prelude to sex, not to comfort them with every intention of stepping away.

"Want a drink?" he asked, only half joking since she looked like she could use one.

Hannah laughed against him in response to his question. She pulled back and glanced up at him. "Yes, actually."

"That's easy enough. Come on inside." With a hand on her shoulder, he walked her inside, trying not to notice how perfectly she fit beneath his arm.

In the kitchen, the microwave dinging told him dinner was ready. He tipped his head toward the table. "Have a seat. I'll get that."

"Okay." She dropped into the chair without argument.

Any other day, she would have jumped to get the food, or set the table, or wash the glass still in the sink from his lunch. Not today.

The wheels of Cooper's brain spun with possible scenarios that could have put Hannah in this mood. He could only imagine what it was. Whatever this accident had entailed, it must have been bad to rattle her, the most grounded woman he'd ever met.

He moved to the cabinet and took down two glasses and the bottle of bourbon. Not knowing if she was a hard-liquor drinker or not, he took the pitcher of sweet tea out of the fridge and put it on the table with the bottle and glasses. Not too bad for a last-minute attempt at hospitality.

"Ice?"

She eyed the bottle and then cut her gaze up to him. "I don't know. Do I need it?"

If she didn't know if she took ice or not in her drink, she definitely wasn't a bourbon drinker.

"Yeah. You do." He took over making her drink, filling the glass with ice and tea and just a finger of the bourbon. Enough to take the edge off but not to get her drunk.

After a swish with a spoon to mix the contents, he set the drink in front of her. Cooper considered pouring a shot for himself too but didn't. He had a feeling he'd need his wits about him to get her over whatever this was.

Instead, he went to the microwave. One touch told him the food was hot enough to eat, so he pulled out the two plates, each with a piece of lasagna. Turning toward the table, plates in hand, he saw Hannah taking a sip from the glass.

He put the plates down. "Drink okay?"

She tipped her head. "Yeah. Not bad actually."

He laughed as he turned for the drawer and grabbed two forks. "Glad to hear it. Now eat up."

"I'm not very—"

"Make me happy. Just take one bite."

She raised her gaze to his. "Is this payback for the other day when I made you eat that stew?"

"Not at all. I don't want you getting into a wreck because I gave you a drink on an empty stomach and then let you drive home." That scenario cut a little too close to home. He shrugged it off. "Of course, I guess if you don't wanna eat and you do drink too much, you could just stay here for the night."

He was only half-joking with that suggestion too.

She glanced at the bottle and then back to him. "I might have to consider that offer."

Cooper raised a brow. He wanted nothing more than Hannah in his bed. He also feared nothing more.

There would be no having sex and kicking her out, never to be seen again the moment they were done. Being with Hannah that way would change absolutely everything between them. They'd become what? A couple?

Or would they become so awkward around each other they'd avoid contact, just when it was starting to feel as if they were friends?

He didn't have many friends. Definitely not enough to lose her as one.

Friends with a female—Cooper had never gone that particular route with a woman before. Now he knew why. He wanted to fuck his friend more than anything else in the world, and to hell with worrying about the fallout or the aftermath.

But with this woman, he had to worry. The stakes seemed higher. The risks greater.

"Eat, Hannah." It would be safer for both of them.

She drew in a deep breath and then let it out, but he was happy to see her stab her fork into the food on the plate.

Cooper followed her lead and jabbed his own fork into the cheesy slice, watching her take one bite and then lay her fork down.

He knew the food was tasty, so that wasn't the problem. Whatever had happened today was. What he didn't know was how to fix it.

"So, Saturday is Skeeter's event, right?" He knew the answer already, but he needed to get her mind off work.

Hannah glanced up. "Yeah."

"You still trying to switch shifts so you can go?"

"I was going to ask the woman I work with today, but things got crazy and I never got around to it."

He nodded. His attempt at small talk had only reminded her of her bad day, proving Cooper should stick to what he was good at rather than venture into unknown territory. Time to get back to what he knew.

"Drink up."

She huffed out a short laugh. "You trying to get me drunk?"

He smiled. "Maybe."

Not really. But he had no idea what else to do to ease her troubles.

Hannah took another small bite of food and then eased her fork down to rest it on the edge of the plate. "A school bus overturned. It was filled with first graders."

First grade. The kids on that bus would have been young. Real young. He figured a few years younger than Skeeter had been the first time Cooper had met him. The reason for her distress was beginning to become clear.

"I'm sorry to hear that."

"Yeah. It was bad." She drew in a wobbly breath. "They brought them in at the start of my shift. We worked on them all day. We lost the driver and one of the children. I was holding the child's hand when . . ." She swallowed hard. "Cooper, it was horrible. His parents—God, they just crumbled at the news."

She shook her head, the shine of unshed tears making her eyes glisten like diamonds.

"Hannah, I'm so sorry." He stood and moved around the table. Biting her lip, she avoided eye contact so he squatted in front of her chair. "Hey. Look at me."

When she glanced up, one tear streamed down her cheek. He took her hands in his. "I'm sure y'all did everything you could."

"It wasn't enough." Her voice shook and he knew she was about ready to break.

Not knowing what to say he stood, drawing her up and

out of her chair. Words weren't his thing anyway. He wrapped his arms around Hannah, pulled her close and held her tightly against him.

He'd expected her to sob, but she didn't. She just clung to him, still and quiet, and he'd never felt so helpless. "Tell me what you need me to do, darlin'."

"Nothing. Just be here with me."

"A'ight. I can do that." Leaning low, he pressed a kiss to the top of her head.

When she pulled back and tilted her head up enough that she could look at him, he saw the need in her eyes. A need that mirrored his own long-banked burning desire for this woman.

A craving that strong did something to a man's mind. It overrode common sense. Made it seem as if things he knew were wrong might just be all right this one time.

He dipped his head lower, hesitating just shy of her lips. A kiss would comfort her. Hell, they'd already kissed and he'd been able to stop himself then. He'd stop himself again now.

"Hannah, tell me the last thing in the world you want me to do is kiss you and I'll back off."

She shook her head, the tiniest of motions as her eyes remained focused on his. "I can't tell you that. It's not true."

Cooper drew in a breath as he closed the final distance. Eyes on her until he pressed his lips to hers, he kissed her like he'd imagined doing so many times over the past few days.

It wasn't the right time. Of course not. She was upset. She'd watched a child's life slip through her fingertips today.

It wasn't good for him either. As much as he wanted her, as much as his resolve waffled, he still knew she needed a better man than him for the long term. He wasn't about to take advantage of her in the here and now, knowing there was no future for them.

Still, he didn't want to stop. His eyes drifted shut as he sank into Hannah's kiss. He tasted the sweet tea and bourbon on her tongue. Felt the soft curves of her pressed against him. Loved the feel of her body beneath her scrubs, warm beneath his hands.

The way Hannah responded, it seemed she didn't want him to stop either. She held tighter and worked his lips, even as his thoughts spiraled. He needed to end this ill-advised kiss, sit down and finish this meal, and then send her home... to do what? Stew in her misery? He didn't like that plan.

He'd keep her there then, but it would be platonic. One friend being there for another. It might kill him, but he'd do it.

Cooper pulled back from the enticement of her lips. Then took the next difficult step of unwrapping his arms from around her and stepping back.

Taking a bracing breath, he pulled his chair farther from the table and sat. "Sit, Hannah. Eat up. It'll make you feel better. I'm betting you didn't get to eat today."

"No, I didn't." She didn't sit in her chair as he expected. Instead, she moved toward his. Facing him, Hannah straddled his legs and sat, right there in his lap.

His cock got impossibly hard in reaction to her weight on him. "What are you doing, darlin'?"

Hannah wrapped her arms around his neck and moved in, her face so close he felt the warmth of her breath. "I think you can figure that out."

"Yeah, I think I can." He wanted those lips against his again.

More than that, he wanted to slide into her and take what they'd both wanted for years. For a fucking decade. Here, like this, he couldn't remember even one of the reasons he'd had for denying them both.

Cooper slid his hands beneath her ass and stood, lifted her with him. She wrapped her legs around his waist as he strode to the bedroom. At least the sheets were clean. He even had condoms in the drawer for those couple of times during the past year or two he'd left the solitude of the cocoon he'd created for himself and gone out seeking the company of a woman.

Thinking of those other faceless, nameless females who'd

passed through his life put the brakes on Cooper's single-minded trajectory toward having her. He laid her on the bed but remained kneeling above her. "You sure you want this?"

"Yes."

"Hannah, you're reacting to a bad day. You're not thinking clearly."

"If that's true, then what was my excuse ten years ago in the front seat of my car?"

"That's easy. I was obviously irresistible back then." He laughed, hoping to joke his way out of a situation he wasn't sure he had the strength to walk away from.

She didn't laugh at his attempt at humor. Instead, she cupped a palm on each side of his face and pulled him closer. If she kissed him again, he'd be lost. He'd take her like he'd wanted to for far too long.

"Cooper. Please."

Those two words, spoken from those lips he'd tasted and wanted more of, broke him. He closed the remaining distance and crashed his mouth against hers.

Thrusting his tongue between her lips, he kissed Hannah with a feral need to finally claim her. To possess all of her. She responded by angling her head and wrapping her arms around his waist.

Cooper rolled to the side just enough so that he could get his hand between them. He slid his fingers beneath the waistband of her scrubs. He traveled over the heat of the bare skin of her belly to slip his fingers beneath the edge of her panties, groaning when he felt her wet heat.

How good it would be to slide inside this woman who already wanted him. Who was already ready for him.

She dragged in a shaky breath and her eyes lost all focus. It seemed a struggle for her to keep them open. She lost the battle and her lids drifted closed.

Damn, there was nothing more beautiful than a woman about to come. Hannah had that look about her now and he'd barely touched her. Her whole body braced for release from the sensations he'd caused with one touch of his hand.

He could have her coming apart in seconds—with his hand, with his mouth, with barely the whisper of a touch—but after all the years he'd resisted the attraction between them, he wasn't about sit back and watch her enjoyment as an outside observer.

Why waste her first orgasm with him on foreplay when he could be a bigger part of it?

Cooper gripped the waistband and yanked her pants down, all the way off her legs. They got caught on her shoes and he had to concentrate long enough to pull them off before he could finish the job of getting Hannah naked.

Her shoes and pants landed on the floor, followed shortly by her lacy underwear, but Cooper forced himself to not slide inside her the moment he bared her from the waist down. He wanted all of her soft warm skin against his.

Apparently, so did she. Hannah struggled to sit up and yanked her top over her head before she reached behind her for the clasp of her bra. He took that opportunity to get himself naked, flinging boots and clothes until there was nothing between them.

Hannah's gaze dropped to his ready cock before she focused on his face. There was no hesitation in her expression, no doubt, nothing but pure need. Open desire.

Reaching for the drawer of the bedside table, Cooper grabbed a condom from the stash that was probably nearing its expiration date at this point. He tore into the packet and covered himself, all while very aware that Hannah was watching him from beneath lids heavy with desire.

His arms shook as he moved to brace over her. He wrote that off to the fact that he'd fought his need for this woman for too long.

He'd made it a lifelong practice to take what he wanted, when he wanted it, whatever that happened to be. Anything and everything. Except for Hannah—until now. No more waiting.

Braced between her legs, Cooper hooked his hands beneath Hannah's knees and plunged inside her. Sinking into her tight, wet heat stole his breath.

The sensation was all encompassing, narrowing his world to only him and her and the place where they were joined.

The realization that she'd gasped as he'd plunged hard and fast into her crept through the haze clouding his brain. Reason returned and he forced himself back to reality long enough to make sure she was all right.

One glance at her face gave him the answer. Hannah's head was pressed back into the pillow, her mouth open and her eyes closed.

Barely thinking himself, he still had the presence of mind to know this was not the face of a woman in pain. This was the expression of a need long denied finally about to be sated, for both of them.

Drawing in a deep breath, he felt the enormity of this one act. It sent a flutter of mingled fear and anticipation through his chest, all the way down to his balls as his body tightened.

He'd regret this the moment he was finished. He knew that with complete certainty. But right now they'd reached the point of no return, so he might as well make sure they both enjoyed it.

Cooper pulled back and then pushed inside again, forcing another open mouthed gasp from Hannah.

She was so beautiful moving beneath him. Not a nurse. Not a waitress. Not a mother. Here and now, Hannah was simply a woman.

He cupped her neck with one palm as he reared back and plunged forward again, rocking her beneath him.

She took every stroke with a bowing of her spine, her body gripping his every time he withdrew, as if she wanted to hold on to him and never let him go.

He ran his hand from her throat to her chest, brushing his thumb over the pebbled peak of one breast before he traveled down the curve of her waist.

There he gripped her hips with both hands, raised her off the bed and began to love her in earnest. He didn't want this to end. Definitely not before he felt Hannah come around him.

She wrapped her legs around his waist as he moved over her, his hands beneath her ass putting her at the perfect angle while he thrust into her.

Every downward stroke elicited a sound of pleasure from Hannah, making him want to repeat it again and again.

He might suck at everything else in his life, but this Cooper knew he was good at. He held her hips high and nudged her G-spot with every stroke before he changed the angle. The move had him pressing tightly against her as the friction rubbed her clit.

Her body tightened around his and her breaths quickened. Reaching down, she gripped his ass, digging her short nails into his flesh as she held him close. She was about to tip over the edge of orgasm, and it was going to be amazing, but all Cooper could think was that once wasn't going to be enough.

What the fuck was he going to do about that?

Her cry as her body gripped his so tightly he could barely move broke through his fear. He couldn't think beyond the feel of Hannah coming around him.

Cooper didn't know whether it was the latex or his anxiety about what he'd feel after letting himself finally come with this woman, but he kept going. Kept thrusting into her, through her first climax, pushing her toward another. Her cries grew louder as he worked her into her second orgasm.

As her body convulsed around him, he knew he could easily get lost inside this woman forever. That word, forever, sent the tingle of fear down his spine even as he felt himself reach the point of no return. A few final thrusts and he was done.

The orgasm shook him to the core, bending his spine and dragging a loud uncontrollable sound from deep within him. It was as much a sound of his release as it was of his regret. Because even still buried inside Hannah, as her body clutched his and she gasped for breath beneath him, he was sorry he'd done this.

This couldn't be a one-night stand. Not with her. She was

too fragile. Too damn nice. And if he couldn't fuck her once and then avoid seeing her, that meant only one thing. He was going to keep seeing her. He was going to have to be a man who was deserving of her.

The problem was that when he failed at that, just like he eventually failed at everything in his life, then what?

The thought was more than he could handle. He pulled out and rolled off her. Flat on his back, he stared at the ceiling.

With a satisfied sigh, she followed him to the other side of the bed, laying one arm over his stomach and her head on his chest.

How long he'd wanted her in his bed, and now, he felt as if he was going to crawl out of his skin with the need to get away from her. Not just away from her, away from himself too. From his certainty this was the biggest mistake he'd ever made in his life.

He fought the urge to get out of bed, get dressed, grab his keys and get into the old truck he'd owned for years. The truck that had left him stranded on the side of the road where Hannah had found him. The night all control had started to spiral away from him when it came to her.

Thoughts of that night led directly to memories of Glen, and all the shit that had gone down with him.

Now he could pile his guilt about having sex with Hannah right on top of his guilt about Glen until it felt like it would crush him. Until he could no longer breathe.

For the first time since he'd accepted that she'd come back into his life those few short days ago, Cooper needed Hannah to go away.

CHAPTER TWELVE

"What's up with you?" Jillian's question brought Hannah out of the depth of her thoughts.

"Nothing." Hannah glanced up and shrugged, before trying to focus again on the chart on the desk in front of her. The one she'd been staring at for what seemed like forever but had yet to actually read.

"Hannah. It's not nothing. What's wrong?"

Nursing was not the kind of job she could afford to be distracted during. Maybe if she got it off her chest, she could push all thoughts of Cooper aside. At least for the remainder of her shift.

Giving in to Jillian's persistence, Hannah sighed. "He hasn't called."

"The old flame?"

"Yeah." She didn't bother correcting Jillian that Cooper had never been Hannah's in the past, so technically she didn't think he could be considered her old flame now.

"Did you . . . you know?"

"Have sex with him? Oh yeah." Hannah laughed at Jillian's wide-eyed expression at her answer as well as at her own stupidity.

She should have known better. A man like Cooper was the love-'em-and-leave-'em type.

He'd loved her all right, and now it was time for him to leave. She'd felt him distance himself that night. Still naked and sweaty from their sex, their breathing hadn't even slowed back to normal when he'd rolled off her.

After that, there might as well have been a brick wall between them. There'd been an unmistakable, tangible change. He'd stiffened when she tried to cuddle afterward, his whole body tense as if he couldn't wait for her to get out of his bed. So she'd left . . . and cried the whole drive home.

That had been two days ago. She'd obsessed over her cell phone the whole next day, and when it didn't ring, she'd done what she'd promised herself she wouldn't do. She'd called him. He didn't answer. It went to voice mail and her certainty increased. She'd never see him again.

He'd told her once those many years ago that she needed to believe a man when he told her the truth about who he was. She'd never believed Cooper when he'd told her he wasn't the one for her.

Maybe she'd have to believe him now that he'd proved it.

"Hannah."

She glanced up at Jillian. "Yeah?"

"There are good men out there."

Hannah let out a short, bitter laugh. "Are there?"

"Yup." Jillian nodded. "But finding one can be a lot like buying new jeans. You might have to try on a dozen pair that fit badly before you find the one perfect pair. Ones that make you feel good. That you'll want to keep forever."

"So one down, eleven more to go?" Two down if Hannah counted her disastrous marriage as well as her insane involvement with Cooper as part of her search for perfect number twelve.

Even so, she didn't think she had it in her to go through this pain again even once. Certainly not nine more times.

Jillian shrugged. "Maybe not. Because sometimes you might find a pair that pinch a little at first, but after you wear them a few times and break them in, you discover that they're the perfect fit."

Hannah laughed at the idea of breaking in Cooper. "Okay, Jillian."

She wasn't sure she believed that any man could be truly changed, especially not at Cooper's age. What was deep inside would remain.

The only question left was who'd been right all those years ago? Her, for seeing the good beneath the bad-boy exterior? Or him, warning her he really was as bad as he tried to act?

She supposed time would tell. She only hoped the wait for one of them to be proven right didn't kill her. Hannah drew in a breath and went back to the file.

"What are you still doing here anyway?" Jillian asked.

"What do you mean? I'm working."

Jillian glanced pointedly at the clock on the wall. "Your shift ended half an hour ago. You know, when I arrived to relieve you."

"I know." She sighed and flipped the file closed. "Need me to stay and help out?" she asked. When all else failed her in life, she always turned to work.

"No. I need you to go home and relax. Treat yourself to a well deserved night off."

Sitting in her empty house waiting for her phone to ring didn't feel like much of a treat, but putting off going home wouldn't change that.

Hannah drew in a breath and closed the file folder. "Okay."

In the car on the drive home Hannah's cell phone rang. Her heart leapt at the sound. A glutton for punishment, her first thought was that it had to be Cooper.

One glance at the caller ID had her hopes sinking. That feeling was quickly replaced by guilt. No mother should be disappointed that her son was calling. She pocketed that guilt along with all the other emotions she had locked away until she was alone and could let them out.

She pulled herself together, mustered a brighter mood she

didn't feel and answered the call. "Hey, my baby boy."

"Hey, Mom."

Hannah remembered it was the day of the touring pro competition. "How'd you do at the event today?"

"Good. Real good. I covered both my rides." Hearing the happiness in her son's voice helped to raise Hannah's spirits.

"That's great. Working with the guys at Riley's is really helping then."

"Yup, seems it is." Skeeter paused before continuing. "So, uh, Cooper was at the competition today."

Just the sound of his name blew her concentration out of the water. She gripped the steering wheel tighter.

"Was he?" Hannah put on her best innocent act and hoped it didn't sound as obviously false to her son as it did to her own ears.

"Yup."

"That's nice that he came to see you ride."

"Yeah, it was."

Her mind spun with this new revelation. Cooper hadn't called her or answered her call after they'd had sex, but he'd gone to see her son ride. What did that mean?

Hannah realized Skeeter had gone suspiciously quiet on the other end of the call. She rushed to fill in the silence. "I guess since you rode so close to home, it shouldn't be a surprise he came to see you."

"Yup, I suppose. But when I asked how he knew I'd be there, he said you'd told him. Funny thing about it is, you never told me you two talked." The suspicion was evident in Skeeter's tone.

She could not get into this conversation with Skeeter about Cooper. He would hear in her voice that something was wrong, and the dead-last thing she intended to ever do was tell her son she'd had sex with his former teacher.

"Didn't I mention it? It must have slipped my mind to tell you."

"Mmm, hmm. Must have." Skeeter sounded like he knew something more than he was saying.

Paranoia struck. She couldn't continue to lie to her son if Cooper had gone and told him something that would contradict her.

But what could Cooper have said? That they'd seen each other? Shared meals for four days straight?

Certainly not that they'd had what amounted to a one-night stand, even if that was never what she'd intended it to be. She wasn't sure of much lately, but she was certain Cooper wouldn't have told Skeeter that.

"What exactly did Cooper say?" She'd intended the question to sound light. Just run-of-the-mill curiosity. Unfortunately, she feared she'd failed at acting casual.

"Just that you'd talked. Strange though, you forgetting to tell me, since it sounded like you two speak quite a bit. He knew all about our training at Riley's. Even about our yoga class. That must have been some conversation you two had."

"Not really. I'm sorry, did you not want anyone to know about the yoga?" Time to turn the tables on this conversation and focus it away from her and Cooper. "Are you embarrassed about that?"

"No, I'm not embarrassed."

She heard the indignation in his voice and knew it had worked to knock him off the subject of Cooper. Hannah decided to change the topic rather than torture her son further. "So how's Riley doing?"

"Better. I think it was good for her, getting out and seeing she could handle hauling the bulls to the event."

"I'm sure it was." How often had Hannah thrown herself into work to hide from things?

"Mom, I really like her . . . and I'm pretty sure she likes me too."

Her son was talking to her about feelings and girls? She tried to keep the surprise out of her voice as she said, "That's good, baby. I'm happy for you."

"Thanks. But if I need to stay here for longer than I'd planned, you know, to help her run the place after the other guys leave, would you be okay?"

"Of course, I'd be okay. You're a good boy and I love you and miss you when you're gone. But I've told you before, I've taken care of myself for a very long time now."

And the other night she'd had Cooper taking care of the parts she'd neglected . . . right before he stopped answering her calls.

So much for her hope the events of that night would be repeated real soon.

"I know that, Mom, but that's because you had to be alone. But now that I'm not on the big tour anymore—"

"Steven Anderson, you listen to me. You do what you need to do for your career and your girl. Don't you dare change your plans on account of me."

He was quiet for a beat. "Okay, but I'm not that far away. I can drive home if you ever need me, or just to visit."

"That's fine. I'd like a visit once in a while." Hannah recalled how many evenings she'd spent having dinner at Cooper's, followed shortly by some pretty vivid, visceral memories of what he'd recently done to her body. There was a slim chance he could come around for a repeat one day, and the thought of Skeeter walking in on that scene horrified Hannah. "Just be sure to call first . . . you know, to make sure I'm not working."

God help her, she was setting in place a plan in case Cooper came over for a booty call. One night with the man and she'd gone crazy, lowering her expectations for him—for them—to pretty much rock bottom.

It was becoming apparent she'd take Cooper any way she could have him, accept as little as he was willing to give, even if it broke her heart.

Her son laughed. "Well, unless you changed the locks on me, if you're working I can let myself in and wait on you."

"Of course, you could. I just don't want you to waste time waiting around when you could be doing other things."

"Uh-huh." He paused again.

She had a feeling he wasn't buying her act and knew something was up. Hannah needed a change of subject once again. "So, tell me about you and Riley. Are you two officially dating yet?"

Maybe it wasn't in the cards for her to be happy in a relationship, but she could at least hope her son was. She was no good with men, but she was a good mother and she could read her only child like an open book. He liked Riley.

If she wasn't mistaken, Skeeter would soon admit to himself, to his girl, and to her and the world that he loved Riley.

That was fine with Hannah. Even if she did nothing else, she'd make sure her son, the only person who loved her, didn't repeat her mistakes.

She'd screwed up royally. By loving Cooper. By waiting ten years for him. By having sex with him. But Skeeter wouldn't live a lifetime of loneliness like she had. She'd see to that if it was the last thing she did.

Then, after he was settled, what would she do with herself? The emotions and the misery of having Cooper and then losing him were too fresh for her to think about that.

She needed to move on one day, but not today. Today she intended to wallow in her pain. Somehow it seemed preferable to feeling nothing at all.

CHAPTER THIRTEEN

Cooper had demons he needed to wrestle. Bad shit from his past. Shit he'd hoped would stay buried. But now he knew the only way to get over it—to move past it—was to face it all.

That he had to do on his own, without Hannah and the stars in her eyes watching him. He couldn't see her until after this was done and his head was on straight again. Then, maybe, he could hope to make some sort of go with her.

He knew what he had to do. He had to make peace with the past before he could move on to his future, and he'd start on that today. He slowed the truck and read the address off the paper.

This was it. Glen's house.

Cooper had sold every last head of stock on the ranch to sever the partnership, and he'd gladly done it to get Glen out of his life. Then, he'd even thrown in a couple of thousand dollars extra to help with the hospital bills. Guilt money, he supposed. Trying to buy himself a clear conscience over the accident.

After that, with not much potential for earning the big payouts on the circuit and no income from the ranch, Cooper had been living off what little savings he had left.

It looked as if Cooper's future had gotten Glen a damn nice place to live. Of course, Glen had also been living with permanent physical damage for the past five years. Ever since that night he'd been driving drunk and upset because Cooper had thrown him out of the house.

Being there, knocking on Glen's door, brought to the surface the guilt he'd buried deep.

As his former partner opened the door, the surprise clear in his features, Cooper said, "Hey."

Glen let out a short, breathy laugh. "Hey. Wasn't expecting you."

"No shit." Cooper swallowed away the dryness. "Can we talk?"

"Yeah. Sure." Glen turned sideways to let Cooper walk past and into the living room.

He noticed how Glen's movements were stiff, and how he favored one leg when he moved to shut the door. The damage from that night hadn't healed completely, and after all this time, Cooper knew it never would. That night had caused Glen to have to make sacrifices of his own too.

"Sorry to drop in like this unannounced."

"Hey, baby." The sound of a man's unfamiliar voice had Cooper turning. The guy, probably a few years older than Cooper and starting to turn gray, stopped in the doorway in the back of the room. "Oh, I didn't realize we had company."

Baby? That endearment from another man, accompanied by the "we" had Cooper turning to Glen for an introduction. An explanation. Something.

Glen drew in a deep breath. "David, this is Cooper Holbrook. Coop, this is my uh, friend David."

David's brows rose high and he looked as if he'd tasted something bitter at Glen's use of the word *friend* in the introduction.

"David, can um, Coop and I have a minute alone?" With that request, Glen ended the stare-off Cooper had somehow become involved in. The man who was obviously Glen's boyfriend didn't look happy about that request.

"Sure. Call me if you need me." The angry, almost jealous expression on the man's face told Cooper a bit more about their relationship.

Cooper had been the object of female jealousy before, but this was his first experience with it from a male.

He watched David leave the room and then turned to Glen. "So . . ."

Glen moved his gaze to the door David had left through and nodded. "Yeah."

Not a lot of words were spoken out loud, but they didn't need more. They both knew the deal. There wasn't anything more to say. Glen had obviously come out of the closet and was openly dating, if not living with a man.

Surprisingly, Cooper didn't find himself all that shocked about it.

He guessed he shouldn't be. It was this—Glen's sexuality—that had wrecked the friendship, the partnership and Glen five years ago.

Memories he'd long ago buried deep surfaced and hit Cooper hard. Glen's girlfriend suggesting they have a threesome. Coop letting his depression over his impending retirement from riding convince him that was a good idea. That fateful night when Glen had leaned over and kissed him . . . and Cooper's reaction to it as he tossed his former friend and partner out of his house and his life only to find out later about the accident that had nearly killed Glen.

Enough time had passed he was happy now that Glen had found someone, man or woman didn't matter. He wasn't there to check on Glen's love life or living arrangements. Cooper was there to apologize and set things right after far too many years had passed.

Apologies didn't come easy to Cooper. He needed to ease into it. "I'm real glad to see you walking so well."

"Yeah. Thanks. All it took was a few months in a wheelchair and six month's physical therapy and hell, I'm almost good as new. You know, except for the plate and pins they put in me." The sarcasm in Glen's voice was clear.

Cooper had heard the details about the accident. He couldn't avoid it. After Darla had called from the hospital, he'd gone back to the house. The Arkansas state police had called Glen's home of record, trying to notify next of kin. What they got was the house phone at the ranch and Cooper, still shell-shocked at the news Darla had dropped on him.

He'd looked up the number for Glen's sister and given it to the cops, but that was it. Cooper hadn't visited Glen in the hospital, even with as bad as they'd told him Glen's condition was.

Instead, he'd boxed up all of Glen's stuff and put it in a storage unit. He'd prepaid for three months and given the sister the combination to the lock.

At the time, he'd thought he was being generous. Now, it all seemed pretty inhuman. Glen had been his best friend for half of his life. Nothing should have been able to change that. Nothing at all. Not even what had happened that night.

He never did find out what exactly had caused the wreck or why Glen was speeding down the highway. It was probably the same reason why Cooper had hid in his parked truck by the lake. They'd both needed to escape that night.

The whys and hows were no longer important, but this apology was. Even if Glen didn't accept it, Cooper still had to make it. Then, after this was over, he could go to Hannah's with a clear conscience. Or at least clearer than before. He had a feeling he'd never be totally free of the guilt of his actions.

Cooper steeled himself and did what he should have done years ago. "Look. I'm sorry. I overreacted then. You were driving that night because of me. The accident was my fault. I'm no good at apologies, and this is long, long overdue. I'm sorry for that too. I'm sorry for everything."

"It's okay, Coop."

"No, it's not." Cooper shook his head even though Glen had sounded sincere. "You could've been killed. Or crippled for life, all because of me. Because I—"

"Flipped out because your best friend, who you'd thought was straight, kissed you?" Glen let out a breath. "Coop, I don't blame you for that."

"It was a fucking shock, but still, I should have handled it better." Cooper glanced in the direction Glen's boyfriend had walked. "So, were you always . . . gay? The whole time?"

One corner of Glen's mouth lifted in a half smile. "I'm not even sure I am now. Not totally anyway. I like having sex with women, Coop. I really and truly do. Always have and I think I always will, even if David hates that I do. Really hates it, with a passion. It's just, I . . ."

"You like penis too." Cooper thought he was being pretty forward thinking, discussing this openly, calmly. He sure didn't expect Glen to laugh in his face.

"Yeah, I guess you could put it that way."

"And back then, when we were partners, did you . . ." Cooper was finding choosing the right words hard. He didn't want to offend Glen but his need to know trumped that.

"Had I ever been with a man?" Glen finished the sentence for him.

Cooper swallowed and nodded. "Yeah."

"Yeah. Not often, but once in a while."

"When?" They had spent so much time together, how had Cooper missed this?

"It wasn't that hard. If you were busy with a girl in your truck, I'd hook up with one of the guys. An anonymous blow job behind a trailer would take the edge off, satisfy that craving for a while, and then I could go back to girls and be happy."

"Jesus." Cooper ran a hand over his face. "I never had any idea."

"Of course not. I didn't want you to know, so I hid it."

"Why?"

"Because I knew you wouldn't handle it well."

He would have handled it better if Glen hadn't freaking kissed him out of the blue. Would he have not freaked out as bad if he'd known the man swung that way? Maybe. Then again, maybe not.

Cooper let out a breath. "That makes me feel better, actually, that you were with other men."

"It does?" Glen looked as surprised as he sounded. "Why?"

Cooper shrugged. "All these years, I've wondered if it was me giving off some sort of vibe that made you think you could . . . Anyway, it's a relief to know it wasn't me. It was you. It's just who you always were."

Glen shook his head. "Spoken like a true homophobe. No, Coop, don't worry. You don't give off a gay vibe. You're as hetero as they come. Like I told you that night, I was drunk. You'd said yes to the threesome after never wanting that before. We were next to each other on the sofa watching TV—"

"A'ight. I got it. I remember." Cooper threw his hand up to stop Glen's recap of the night he remembered too well, the one night he would never forget. It didn't prevent him from finishing the unspoken end of Glen's sentence in his head. *Watching the TV with their pants off and their hands on their dicks.* "And I guess that situation could have been confusing."

So confusing it had taken Glen's tongue in his mouth plus his hand reaching for Cooper's dick before he had sobered up enough and had the presence of mind to stop the situation.

Maybe half the anger had come from Cooper's own fears. What if he'd been drunker? Would he have let Glen—

Cooper yanked his mind away from the what-ifs. They didn't change or help anything. "Anyway, I came to tell you I was sorry, and to tell you that you were right about something else back then."

"Oh really? I was right about something? You don't say that all that often, so now I'm extra curious." Glen crossed his arms and leaned back against the wall. "Tell me, what was I right about?"

"I'm kind of seeing Hannah now. You remember, Skeeter's mother. The kid I used to—"

"I know who he is and who she is. About damn time,

Coop, but I guess better late than never."

"Yeah. You're right. I should have listened to you and asked her out back then."

"Yup." Glen dipped his head. "You should have."

Cooper had to wonder what would have happened differently if he had been dating Hannah ten, or even five years ago.

If he had been, there would have been no talk of a threesome with Glen and Darla, that's for damn sure. Glen would likely have continued to keep his extracurricular activities of the male variety on the down low. He would have never kicked Glen out and dissolved what by now could have been one hell of a stock business. He'd have plenty of money and a well-run ranch.

Absolutely everything would have been different for Cooper, but it would have been different for Glen too. He wouldn't have a permanent limp, but he also would have been living half a life. He'd probably still be pretending to be straight, hiding parts of who he was to fit into Cooper's ideal world instead of how things were now. Glen openly with David as a couple.

"You happy?" Cooper's question had Glen hesitating before he lifted one shoulder. Glen's shrug confused Cooper. "What's wrong? You've got a nice boyfriend. You've got a nice house."

Glen glanced at the doorway David had left through. "Things are all right. I wouldn't say they're good."

Something Glen had said before came back to Cooper. "Because he doesn't like having sex with women and he hates that you do?"

Glen smiled. "Yeah, that's part of it, among other things. But besides the relationship, I hate living in town. There's too many neighbors too damn close. I hate working at the feed store. I'm the manager, but still, it's not like working for myself alongside you when we could be outside and tending to the animals. The work was hard, but it was satisfying, you know? Now all I handle is paperwork and annoyed customers."

Cooper nodded, understanding so much of that himself. He kept the ranch—broken as it was—and all the acreage because he couldn't tolerate city life or neighbors too close.

Not wanting to work for someone else was one reason he lived like a pauper. Rather than get a real job and make more money he survived off the meager remains in his bank account and the tiny residual income from the few products he'd lent his name to back when his name was worth something.

But he wouldn't have to live hand to mouth if he started up the business again. "I still own the farm, free and clear. I don't have a mortgage on it, but I also don't have any stock."

"I heard. You miss it?"

"Yeah. I wouldn't mind starting business back up and maybe taking on a partner." He brought his eyes up to meet Glen's.

Glen opened his mouth and then closed it again before he started the process over again and words finally came out. "What are you saying, Coop?"

"That I want to give it another go with you and me—" He realized how that sounded and rushed to add, "The business, not the uh, other stuff."

"Yeah, I got that, but thanks for spelling it out." Glen rolled his eyes.

"You think you could handle the work?" Cooper eyed Glen's leg.

"I think so. I might not walk so pretty or move as fast as I used to, but the leg's strong. And I've seen you tend the stock when you were way more broken up than me."

Cooper couldn't argue Glen's point about that.

"You could move back in. And it wouldn't be like before. I don't want you hiding shit from me. You bring a woman home to your bed, fine. You bring David, or any other guy home, that's fine too."

"You'd be okay with that?" Glen looked pretty doubtful.

Cooper didn't blame him. He thought for a second before

nodding. "Yup. I think I would. It'd be wrong of me to have you sneaking around and trying to hide who you are."

He might consider busting open the wall between his and Glen's bedrooms and adding a nice thick layer of insulation as soundproofing, but otherwise, he really thought he could handle it. Cooper was confident he'd matured, mellowed with age.

"You sure you want me living there? Hannah and you, won't you want your privacy?"

Cooper shrugged. "I'll give you your privacy, you give me mine. Just like it always was."

Glen dipped his head. "But what if you two get serious and want to get married?"

"Married?" Cooper's voice cracked on the word. "Jesus, Glen, you trying to run me off?"

He and Hannah had had sex once. He needed time to wrap his head around things like love and marriage.

Yeah, that one time with her had been amazing, but it had also scared the shit out of him.

That was one reason he'd avoided her since then. He had to get his bearings. He also wanted things made right with Glen. He wanted to be heading in the right direction for his future before he talked to her again.

But truth be told, if he could see himself married to any woman, it would be to Hannah.

Glen smiled. "You like her. I can tell."

"Yeah, I do. But let me get through a few of the important firsts with her before you put a ring on my finger. Like a real date. A'ight?"

Glen smiled. "I remember you saying back then that you fucked women, you didn't date them."

"I know, and shut up if you're only going to say I told you so. I don't need to hear it. I was an idiot when it came to Hannah."

"You're admitting that? Now I know this is serious. I'll be hearing wedding bells before you know it. Though I guess there's enough acres you two could take the house and I could build myself a little place off to the side. Maybe a trailer for the time being."

"Yes, you could if you want, but only if you stop talking about me and marriage. A'ight? Quit, or I'm taking back the offer."

Still, Cooper had to admit that Glen painted a nice picture. A thriving ranch. His partner and best friend steps away in his own place. Hannah playing house with him as a real couple. Everyone happy.

Damn. Now that he thought of it, he wanted it, which made him even more scared that it was all beyond his grasp.

"I've been avoiding her for two days because I'm so afraid I'm going to fuck things up. I needed to get my head on straight before I see her again. I want it to be serious with her, and that scares the shit out of me."

Glen laughed. "Oh, I believe it. But I think you're off to a good start."

"How's that?"

"Because you're taking the time you need to actually think rather than just barreling in headfirst like you used to. Because being with her made you want to clean up a mess that you never bothered with for near five years."

It was all true. Because of Hannah he'd cleaned up the messes both at the ranch and in his life. "I miss having you around to talk to."

The corner of Glen's mouth lifted. "Me too."

"You'll consider my offer?" As much as he wanted everything to be right with Hannah, Cooper wanted things with Glen to work out too. All of it. The partnership and the friendship.

Glen tipped his head in a nod. "I will."

Coop glanced out the back door where Glen's main squeeze—his man-friend, which was as good a term as any—was manning the grill while shooting possessive, jealous-looking glances at the house. "I don't know what the living situation is here, but know you're welcome at my place. If he's not the right one for you, ditch him. You deserve someone who makes you happy."

Glen nodded. "Thanks. But remember, so do you."

"Yeah. I think I finally get that."

"About damn time." Glen smiled.

"Yeah, I know. I guess I'm a slow learner. A'ight. I'm gonna go. Hannah should be home from work by now." He turned to the door but glanced back, his hand on the knob. "You'll have to bring your television with you if you move back. I never got around to buying myself one."

Glen laughed. "Okay."

Things were far from back to normal, but this was a good start.

CHAPTER FOURTEEN

Hannah pulled into the driveway after hanging up with Skeeter and slammed on the brakes as her heart began to pound. Cooper's truck was in the drive.

The truck's door swung open and Cooper stepped out. It was all she could do to function enough to pull the car up to the curb. Even then, she almost forgot to put the transmission in park. She only noticed when she tried to pull the key out of the ignition and the mechanism wouldn't let her.

Jeez, she had it bad. She'd been driving for twenty-five years but couldn't manage the simple task now because Cooper was there. There to see her. And he was smiling.

She managed to get both her keys and herself out of the car as he walked toward her. She'd just slammed the door when she found herself pressed up against it, pinned between Cooper's body and the vehicle.

He grabbed the back of her neck with one hand and crashed his mouth into hers.

Right out in the open, in view of the street and all her neighbors, Cooper kissed her, thrusting his tongue between her lips.

It was like a public claiming of her as his. He kissed her hard and held her with a possessive grip that left no doubt in her mind. He wanted and needed her as much as she did him.

He stopped kissing her and said, "Let's go inside."

Cooper might have said *inside*, but his eyes said something else. If she wasn't mistaken he wanted to take her inside and to bed.

"Okay." Hannah led the way to the house, Cooper behind her where she hoped he didn't see her hands shaking as she unlocked the door.

Stupid woman that she was, once they were inside she didn't just accept his enticing suggestion and drag him to her bedroom. She had to know something first, so instead she said, "I wasn't sure I'd be seeing you again. When I didn't hear from you—"

He pressed his lips together and nodded. "I know. I wasn't ready. I am now."

"What's changed?"

"Nothing. Everything. All I know is I'm done fighting this thing between us, Hannah. I want you in my life, and not just because I can't seem to keep my hands off you." Looking down at her from beneath heavy lids, he ran his palms down her sides. "You good with that?"

A smile she couldn't control and didn't want to bowed her lips. "Yeah, I'm good."

Grabbing his hand, she tugged him toward her room, but he resisted, holding her back.

"I'm thinking maybe we should talk first."

She turned back to face Cooper. "Talk? Um, sure. We can talk."

He grabbed both of her hands. "Hannah."

"Yeah?"

He was starting to worry her with his seriousness.

"I'm sorry I didn't call."

Relieved that was all that was worrying him, she accepted the apology with a nod. "It's okay."

"No, it's not. But I had some shit to work out first."

Like another woman in his life? She hated that her mind went there, but she couldn't help it. As casually as she could muster, she asked, "Did you get it worked out?"

"I did." He dipped his head and then drew in a breath. "I went to see Glen and talked to him about possibly starting up the stock business again."

Glen. The one piece from Cooper's life that had gone missing without explanation. He wanted to build up the ranch again. That was very good news.

Her suspicions had been for nothing. She blew out the breath she hadn't realized she'd been holding. "Wow. Cooper, that's great."

"I hope so. It's not a done deal yet. He's thinking about it, but I think there's a good chance."

"I'm really happy for you."

He smiled. "I know you are. You always were pleased seeing other folks doing good." He took a step closer. "I shoulda called you the next day. Hell, that night even. I just needed to handle this thing with Glen first. Can you forgive me?"

Hannah had a feeling she'd forgive Cooper for a lot of things. This transgression didn't require much forgiveness. He needed to get his life together, and he'd taken a huge step toward doing that. It didn't mean she couldn't tease him a little.

"I don't know. That depends." She angled her head to the side. "I have to make sure of a few things first."

"Sure. Shoot."

"Are you going to get me all hot and bothered and then walk away from me like you did ten years ago?"

His lips tipped up in a smile. "Oh, darlin', you don't have to worry about that ever again."

"Are you going to answer the phone when I call you?" she continued.

"I promise. I'll answer whenever you call, no matter what." He held up one hand with his pledge.

His promise was good enough for her. She glanced toward

the kitchen. "Fine. Just let me grab a couple of bottles of water from the kitchen. Your making this up to me could take all night and we'll need provisions."

His eyes widened. She ignored his surprise and headed for the fridge.

~ * ~

Hannah's bedroom was filled with things from her everyday life. It was like Cooper had reached the inner sanctum where the private Hannah was exposed, instead of the public persona.

Him being there made things began to feel really real. But unlike in the past, he didn't have the urge to bolt.

Where in the old days he would have itched to turn any personal photos toward the wall, with Hannah he found he wanted to look at the pictures of Skeeter as a baby. Take a closer look at the photos of the older man who must be Hannah's late father and at the picture of a younger Hannah wearing a smile and a baby on her hip.

He didn't have all that much time to look as she led the way toward the bed. It was neat and perfectly made, exactly as he'd imagined it would be. The woman worked two jobs, lived basically alone in the house and still she made her bed. Every morning, he was sure.

She was the opposite of him. That should scare him. Hell, it used to. Not anymore. He'd have to think more about why that was later. Too much thinking was bad for a man.

Cooper waited for her to put the bottled water on the nightstand before he pulled her toward him. She came willingly and he saw a need in her eyes reflecting his own.

He'd done things he wasn't proud of in his past. He had regrets, just like any man. Taking too long to accept he had feelings for Hannah would always remain one of those regrets.

Frightening as it was, he wanted Hannah in his life. Not for a night. Not for a few tumbles in his bed. But forever.

That word—forever—made his chest clench, but he couldn't deny it anymore.

He was definitely done fighting this. It was inevitable, them being together. He only wished he'd been capable of embracing the reality of these feelings years ago. It might have saved them all a heap of pain. Glen too.

Maybe he'd been wrong avoiding this with her all those years ago. Then again, maybe his actions had been right for the man he'd been then. He hoped to God what he was doing now was right.

When he pushed doubt to the side, it left only the raw need dominating him. If he was going to sideline the fear that had ridden him most of his life, he needed to concentrate on something else for a little bit. Making love to Hannah was the perfect solution.

She was right, it might take all night, but he wasn't leaving there until he'd given them both what they'd sampled only once and much too briefly the other night. What they'd been denied for too long.

Cooper ran his hands over her curves. All soft and warm. All woman. All his. His body tightened at the thought.

Her clothes were in the way. He could make them both feel so much better with more freedom to move and there was this nice bed just waiting for them.

"Sit."

She complied without question and the many things he wanted to ask her to do spun in his head. She was so sweet, but damn, he had a feeling she could be bad too, given the right motivation.

Kneeling at her feet, he pulled off her shoes and tossed them to the side. From the same position, he released the drawstring on her scrubs and grasped the elastic waistband.

She braced her weight on her hands and lifted her hips so he could tug the pants down.

Anxious now to get her out of all remnants of the job that consumed so many of her waking hours, he stood and yanked her top off.

She was tempting on a normal day. Hannah in nothing but matching lace panties and a bra took his breath away.

With both hands, he grasped the sides of her underwear and slid them over her hips. She watched him with narrowed eyes as he stripped her panties from her.

The soft lace seemed to weigh nothing in his hand. What was it about women's undergarments that could twist a man's gut in knots? Just holding these made him want to plunge inside her.

It had probably been a bad idea taking them off so soon, but it was way too late to worry about it now. He steeled his resolve and dropped the scrap of lace to the carpet.

Those panties would definitely play a part in his fantasies in future. One night when he was home alone and thinking of her.

Every second with Hannah made him crave a million more.

He pressed against her shoulder easing her back until she was lying flat on the bed. He leaned low and brushed his lips over the pale skin of her thigh.

Using his thumbs to spread her, he flicked his tongue over a spot that had her jumping beneath him. He slid two fingers inside Hannah and she sucked in a breath of air between her teeth in response.

Lifting his head a bit, he saw the pleasure on her face. He watched her eyes roll back and grinned. "Don't pass out, darlin'. You're gonna want to be awake for this."

Cooper didn't know if it was Hannah's responsiveness to his every touch, or just Hannah herself, but he was enjoying pleasing her. It was more fun than he'd ever had with his pants on.

Smiling, he went back to work, his sole goal to please her. It was quite the change for him. Back in the day, once he'd warmed up the woman just enough to get her to do what he wanted with her, his main concern had been getting himself off.

He'd known one taste wouldn't be enough with Hannah, but he did it anyway and was going to do it again, as often as she'd let him. He dipped his head, spread her wide and drove his tongue deep between the folds of her flesh.

She gasped as he connected with the spot he sought. He drew her between his lips and sucked hard enough to elicit a moan from her.

It seemed forever since he'd had his mouth on a woman. It had been a long time since he'd wanted to be this close, this intimate. With Hannah, he couldn't seem to stop himself and didn't want to.

Not opening his jeans and plunging into her was killing him, but he held strong somehow. He'd get to his end goal eventually, but a need this deep, so long in coming, warranted taking his time to satisfy them both.

Hannah writhed beneath him. He realized he'd be happy to do this with her every day and every night. No fear of boredom. No fear of commitment. Just a warmth inside him that chased away the darkness and the cold.

She settled her hands on his head and held him close. She needn't have worried. He wasn't going anywhere anytime soon.

Cooper doubled his efforts and felt her slip over the edge of orgasm as her cries filled the room.

She didn't stop gasping throughout the time it took him to stand up, tear off his clothes and slide on a condom. Then he was back, plunging inside the woman he couldn't get enough of.

Her body welcomed his like it was made for him.

He forced his eyes open and watched her face as he loved her. Her emotions showed clearly and echoed his own. Wonder. Relief. Need.

He'd long ago lost count of how many women he had taken over the course of his lifetime. Some just like this, face to face. Some with far more creativity. Yet the act had never consumed him so completely as it did with Hannah.

Maybe that was the difference that caring about her made.

He tried to last but couldn't. Much too soon, he came with an intensity he'd never felt with any other woman.

The climax seemed to fill him with emotion as much as it

drained him of energy. Unable to hold himself up any longer, he collapsed over Hannah.

Still breathless, he realized he must be crushing her. With his arms locked around her, he rolled to the side and brought her with him.

This time, when the orgasm high began to fade, Cooper didn't have the urge to flee. It was a nice change.

Equally as strange to him was that he wanted to talk. "This isn't just about sex, you know," he said.

"No?" That one word from Hannah felt loaded with so much. Questions. Doubt. Hope.

"No. I . . ." Cooper braced himself and started again. "You deserve someone so much better than me, but I'm working on being a better man, and I'd like it if you were around for it."

"I'd like that too." As Hannah's cheek rested against his chest he felt her smile. He blew out a breath in relief.

"Good." Now that the hard stuff was out of the way, he realized he'd never told her about seeing her son. "So I went to the competition and saw Skeeter."

"Yeah, about that." She lifted her head and he saw the humor in her expression. "You got me in trouble."

"I did? How?"

"He's suspicious of us now. You knew too much about what he's doing, and since I hadn't told him we were seeing so much of each other, never mind doing anything else together, he thought it was odd. He suspects."

Cooper shrugged. "So? Is that a problem?"

"That my son might have guessed his teacher and I are having sex?" Her eyes widened as she hissed out the last word, as if Skeeter would be able to hear if she said it too loudly. "Yes, it's a problem."

He couldn't help but chuckle at her reaction. "Well, you'd better get over it. I don't intend on hiding our relationship from anybody, particularly not the most important person in your life. He's a grown man. He'll deal with it."

She looked so horrified at the concept, Cooper smiled as

he pulled her closer and wrapped his arms around her. "It'll be okay, Hannah. Besides, even if we don't tell him, he'll figure it out eventually. The minute he sees us together at the bull-riding clinic."

Hannah pulled back. "What bull-riding clinic?"

"I had an idea. It seems I was a pretty good teacher way back when. I thought maybe I could be again. I talked to Skeeter about it and he thinks it's a good idea."

"So do I. You were an amazing teacher."

Cooper shrugged. "I don't know about that, but good enough people might be willing to come if I set up some classes. Skeeter said he'd help me out if I set up a group class on a day he wasn't competing. Like an intensive weekend, maybe once a month."

Her smile spread wide. "I couldn't be prouder of you."

He waited for the fear to grip him. Her having such blind faith in him had sent him running from her years ago. There was still the residual fear of failure, but it wasn't enough to turn him away from his end goal. In fact, it made him want it all the more.

"Thanks, Hannah. That means a lot."

"And maybe I could help too. All those bull riders will be hungry. I could make a big pot of chili—"

Cooper laughed. "I know you could. That would be great."

He realized nothing had seemed great to him in a very long time, but now it seemed he couldn't stop smiling, laughing. If he didn't watch it, he might become a damn optimist like Hannah, and maybe that wouldn't be so bad.

"I have some news too," she raised her gaze to his.

"Do you? Tell me." He squeezed her closer to him.

"Skeeter called right before I pulled in the driveway to ask if I'd mind if he stayed there and helped Riley run the ranch."

He didn't know shit about raising a child, but he did know how males thought. Skeeter was going to want to lock down that girl and make her his.

"Does that mean what I think it means?" he asked.

"That it might not be all that long before he's asking Riley to marry him?" Hannah drew in a breath and let it out. "I think it might."

He glanced down at her. "How would you feel about that?"

"I hope he's not too young and making a mistake, but I think I'd be okay with it. He likes her a lot and he's happy. I hear it in his voice."

"A'ight then." He dipped his head in a nod. "You know what this means, don't you?"

"That if they do get married, I could easily be a grandmother very soon?" She let out a snort.

"You'd be the hottest grandmother I've ever seen, so don't sound so miserable about it." He squeezed her shoulder. "But no, I was going to say this means with Skeeter settled and happy, you get to work on doing the same for yourself."

"Settled and happy." Hannah blew out a laugh. "I'm not sure I can say I've ever been both at once."

"Yeah. Me either."

"Think it's possible?" she asked.

Cooper figured if it were, it would be possible with her. "I'm up for the challenge. You?"

Her smile beamed. "Yeah. I am."

EPILOGUE

The screen on the back door squeaked open. Hannah glanced at the clock on the microwave while she stirred the pot of chili. "Right on time. Lunch is ready."

"You know I'm never late for one of your meals." Cooper stepped behind her and laid his hands on either side of her waist. He delivered a kiss to her cheek and then pressed his lips to her ear. "I'll deliver a proper thank you for all your hard work tonight."

He moved away quickly after the hushed promise that had her insides bubbling as hot as the chili on the stove.

"Hey, Mom." Skeeter had followed Cooper into the kitchen. "Smells good. I'm starving."

"That's no surprise. You've been working hard." She tipped her head toward the door. "The sweet tea is in the big orange cooler, but I still need to grab the sleeve of plastic cups. It's in the trunk of my car."

"Skeeter, go and get those cups for your mom. Then tell them boys to wash up for lunch."

"Yes, sir."

Hannah smiled as her son pushed through the door to where her car was parked in front of Cooper's house. She turned and stepped into Cooper's arms, wrapping her own around him.

"Mmm, don't get me started." He ran his hands down to her ass with a groan. She felt him hardening against her. "Damn, I've got half a dozen students right outside and I don't want them seeing what you do to me."

"I'm happy to know that I can still do that to you."

"Are you crazy, woman? I don't care if it's been six months or sixty years, I'll never grow tired of you." He dropped a kiss on her lips and then took a step back just as the screen door slammed again and Glen stepped into the kitchen.

His residual limp had improved visibly over the past few months. Cooper had said he thought it was from all the physical work on the ranch making Glen's muscles stronger. Something his managerial job at the feed store hadn't done.

Hannah was simply content to see both men well and happy.

Glen glanced at Hannah. "Need me to carry anything outside?"

"Yes, thank you, Glen. The pot of chili can go out." She shot a look at Cooper who'd done nothing but make her forget about the food and the bull-riding clinic's students waiting for it since walking into the kitchen.

Cooper frowned at her. "What? Don't look at me like that. I'll freely admit Glen's a better man than me. Is it my fault I'm so intoxicated by the love of my life that I forget basic manners when I'm near her?"

Glen smiled and shook his head as he lifted the pot by the handles. "That infamous Holbrook charm always has gotten Coop out of a heap of trouble."

Cooper grinned so wide it crinkled his eyes. "Damn right." He reached past Hannah and grabbed the basket full of corn bread. "I got this."

She shook her head at him for taking the smaller of the two items that had to go out. "Thank you."

"No problem. You can thank me later." He winked and damned if her knees still didn't go weak at the sight, even after having him in her life for all these months.

Once the men had gone out and she was alone in the kitchen, she could gather her wits enough to inventory what more she had to do. She remembered the paper napkins weren't out yet.

Grabbing the stack, she turned for the door just as Riley came in. "Mrs. Anderson—"

"When are you going to stop calling me that? I told you that Hannah is fine."

The girl's cheeks turned pink. "I'm sorry."

"It's all right. But when you and Skeeter finally do get married, I'm really going to put my foot down."

"Yes, ma'am."

Hannah let her gaze drop to the girl's right hand where she wore Skeeter's ring. They'd told her it would stay there until they decided it was time to get officially engaged and then it would move to the proper ring finger. Hannah was just fine with them taking their time.

"Did you need something?" she asked her future daughter-in-law.

"Cooper said to tell you to stop fussing and come out and eat."

Ignoring that he was Cooper while she was still Mrs. Anderson, Hannah smiled. "I'm on my way."

The girl dipped her cowboy hat in a nod and turned for the door as Hannah followed in her wake.

She might look young—hell, she was young—but Hannah had to remember Riley owned and operated one of the top bucking-bull businesses in the country. She was a survivor after all she'd gone through at such a young age. Riley was a good match for Skeeter. No doubt the girl kept him on his toes.

The heat of the sun beat down, but a nice breeze made it bearable as Hannah headed toward the long table set up beneath the shade of the big old oak near the house.

The benches were already lined with boys of various ages and sizes, all of them there to learn what Cooper had to teach. Skeeter too, when he had a break from the pro tour he was now leading in the standings once again.

What a huge difference half a year made. If she let herself think back to how things had been as compared to how they were now, she'd tear up, and this wasn't the time for that.

Instead, she donned a smile and strode to the group.

After dropping the napkins onto the table and securing them from the wind beneath the stack of plates, she dropped a quick kiss on Skeeter's cheek and then turned and delivered a much more intense one to Cooper's lips.

Cooper glanced up, eyebrows raised. "Not that I'm complaining, but what was that for?"

"Just 'cause." She couldn't say more because the tears of happiness were too close to the surface and threatening to break free.

She couldn't tell him it was because she finally had everything she'd always wanted. That against all odds and in spite of both of their pasts, they were settled and happy. That she prayed every night before she fell asleep in his arms that nothing would change because things were nearly perfect the way they were.

He smiled. "A'ight. Feel free to do that just 'cause anytime you want."

Hannah smiled away the tightness of emotion and nodded. "I will. Promise."

It was the easiest promise she'd ever made.

Don't miss the rest of the Studs in Spurs novels for happy endings for all of your favorite heroes!

ABOUT THE AUTHOR

A top 10 *New York Times* bestseller, Cat Johnson writes the *USA Today* bestselling Hot SEALs series. Known for her creative marketing, Cat has sponsored bull riding cowboys, promoted romance using bologna and owns a collection of cowboy boots and camouflage for book signings.

For more visit CatJohnson.net
Join the mailing list at catjohnson.net/news

CPSIA information can be obtained
at www.ICGtesting.com
Printed in the USA
LVHW100823210522
719388LV00019B/240